Hiding Behind The Couch Series

The Advent of Reason

by
Debbie McGowan

Beaten Track
www.beatentrackpublishing.com

The Advent of Reason

Published 2018 by Beaten Track Publishing
Copyright © 2018–2023 Debbie McGowan

Paperback ISBN: 978 1 78645 299 3
eBook ISBN: 978 1 78645 300 6

Cover Design by Debbie McGowan

Beaten Track Publishing,
Burscough. Lancashire.
www.beatentrackpublishing.com

For Jor:

Castle and thunderstorm,
as promised…three years ago.

Thank you so much for *everything*.

Chapter One

I T WASN'T SNOWING...YET, but the Peak District sky was the heavy, dull grey Josh associated with an imminent downpour. It made for striking views and very trying driving conditions; the road was treacherous—narrow, bendy and with a sheer drop on both sides—and the route was unfamiliar, making him thankful, on this occasion only, for the satnav's expert navigation. Two hours' travelling undertaken so far and not a single wrong turn; it was a veritable personal best worthy of celebration, but not before they reached their destination.

As if Josh's thoughts had prompted it, and he couldn't be sure they hadn't, George chose that moment to ask, "Are we nearly there yet?"

Josh laughed and directed George's attention to the ETA on the satnav's screen: another twenty minutes. "Are you bored?"

"Nope, I really don't like this road." George peered out the passenger-side window and whistled a non-tune. His shoulders rose up to almost meet his ears.

"Then don't look," Josh advised. "I'm not."

"Yeah, that's not comforting when you're driving."

Josh sighed and didn't bother explaining that all of his attention was on the road ahead and not on the low-lying grazing land surrounding it or else that was where they'd end up, flipped with wheels spinning in the air, myriad curious sheep the only witnesses to their demise. Hospital was not where he wanted to be five days before Christmas, nor indeed any other time, but especially not when it was their anniversary weekend and this was his gift to George.

"Why don't you put the radio on?" he suggested.

"D'you want it on?"

"I don't mind either way, but it might stop you admiring the view."

"OK." George pressed the power button, tilting his head to listen. "Can I turn it up a bit?"

"Fine with me." Josh usually kept the radio at such a low volume it was barely audible. Then he'd collect Libby from school or a friend's, she'd turn it up, gradually, and he'd notice she was doing it, but it wasn't unbearable—until the next time he got in the car and it near blasted his ears off his head.

Thankfully, George preferred a volume somewhere between the two extremes; the auto-tune settled on a local station, and George settled back in his seat. His relaxed posture lasted no more than three seconds before he and Josh both burst into laughter at the completely unfunny radio ad that was playing.

"Car trouble?" George said, deepening his voice and plumbing up his accent.

"Time for a change?" Josh said in the same kind of accent, which was much like his own, but it wasn't his line anyway.

"Our cars come with nought percent finance…" George began, but he was laughing too much to go on. The script was from a radio ad they knew off by heart, as did all their friendship group, because it was one Kris had made years ago and it was *still* playing on their local station back home.

Giggling, they finished off together, "Duh-buh-duh-buh-duh, duh-buh-duh-buh-duh. Terms and conditions apply," followed by, "Oh shit!" from Josh as he hit the brakes a little too late for the upcoming bend. He steered hard left; the car dropped and tilted as the offside tyres ran through the few inches of long grass next to the tarmac and then righted itself again as all four tyres regained traction on the road. Josh blew his hair back from his eyes and adjusted in his seat, pulse racing from the momentary excitement.

All the while, George clung—and was still clinging—white-knuckled, to the grab handle above his door. They were at least a mile further along the road before he cautiously loosened his grip.

"Another fifteen minutes," Josh placated, taking extra care now, as they descended through a series of increasingly sharp bends sporting black-and-white arrows, into a tiny hamlet consisting of a church and no more than a dozen houses.

"Wow, it's beautiful!" Josh exclaimed.

The hamlet was a life-size replica of the illuminated miniature village currently on display in their living room. The buildings' windows glowed warmly in the dwindling daylight, and all the trees were adorned with colourful lights.

George groaned. "And now it's snowing."

"Is it?" Josh squinted at the specks slanting through the beams from the car's headlights, bright white in the gloom. At first, they were tiny, indiscernible from rain, but soon unmistakeably snowflakes. "Yes, it is," he confirmed. "Perfect!" Nothing glum about his declaration. George muttered something sweary and reinstated his grip on the handle.

"Only twelve more minutes," Josh comforted. They were close enough to their destination for the snow not to hinder them too much, and he was trying not to take George's anxiety to heart. He was generally a very well-behaved passenger, mostly because he hated driving and didn't dare risk any kind of remark that might put him behind the wheel, especially in these conditions, which steadily worsened as they left the village behind and headed once more out onto open moorland. Josh dropped gears as they began to climb another hill and reached across to squeeze George's hand. "We might get a white Christmas at this rate."

"Awesome," George said flatly and placed Josh's hand back on the steering wheel.

"Or at least a white anniversary. Don't you think it's romantic?"

"Not really."

"Well, I think it is. A weekend in a rustic manor house, just the two of us... And yes, I'm aware other people will be there too, but no ferrying Libby to and from friends' houses..."

"Or popping over to see my mum…"

"Or my grandma…"

"No friends dropping in at a moment's notice…"

"Or Sean just walking in and demanding coffee with menaces," Josh added. "See? We'll be positively alone." He reached for George again, gave his arm a very quick squeeze of reassurance and released him so he could drive two-handed, staying quiet as he navigated the next bend in the road and crested a hill. "I'm excited to see what Merton Hall looks like. Oh! Is that it, do you think?"

George followed the direction of Josh's gaze and leaned forward in an effort to see better the dark form sitting just below the horizon. Elongated bright yellow rectangles flared in the snowflakes smeared across the windscreen, making it difficult to gauge how many windows there were exactly, and they were in three rows of seven, maybe eight—certainly more than could be found in an average-sized house or even an entire row.

"How many bedrooms did Gabby say again?" Josh asked.

"Thirty-seven."

"That's an odd number. Not odd…strange. Well, odd, too."

"And a prime number. Wonder if it means anything." George opened the glove box and pulled out a pile of papers. "It's not rustic either. There's a photo of it in the brochure she gave me." He shuffled through until he found the glossy leaflet. "Can't see properly, but yes. I reckon that's it."

"Excellent."

Their journey continued in silence, with both of their attention split between the run of Christmas classics on the radio and the decreasing visibility that had Josh keeping his speed under twenty miles an hour. For the time being, the snow wasn't sticking to the ground, but it was beginning to accumulate in the hawthorn hedges and trees, the last remnants of daylight lending a muted lilac tinge to the westerly aspects of branches and trunks.

"This would make a stunning painting," Josh thought aloud. "I bet you could paint it from memory."

"Probably." George turned a little in his seat. He was gearing up to saying something he thought Josh wouldn't like, and it took him a minute or so to find the words. Eventually, he said, "OK. Truth time."

"OK?"

"Are you actually excited for this weekend or are you just saying it for my benefit?"

"Where did that come from?"

"I've been thinking about it since we left home. I mean…this is an amazing anniversary gift, and I'm not saying we should turn back or anything like that, but it's *our* anniversary and we should both enjoy it."

The satnav directed Josh to take the next right, still a quarter of a mile ahead of them, but he waited until he'd made the turn, carefully planning his response before he gave it. "Truth time?"

"Yep."

"When you told me Gabby's parents were opening their house to the public and you wanted to come here, my first thought was of those guided tours around roped-off rooms seemingly designed for the sole purpose of the filthy rich rubbing poor people's noses in it while said paupers defend the gross inequalities of ascribed status."

"OK," George said with a smirk that Josh couldn't see, but he heard it in his tone.

"What's funny?"

"The social commentary."

"It's true, though, isn't it? Why else would the aristocracy open their homes to commoners?"

"To make money?" George said as if it were wild speculation. "You know it's not going to be like that, don't you?"

"Yes, I know. They've fully opened the house."

"*Most* of the house," George corrected.

"That's to be expected. They don't want us proles peeing all over their hand-woven bathroom rugs and infesting their four-posters with fleas and dysentery."

George sighed. "Gee, this is going to be fun…"

"I will behave impeccably all weekend."

"Is that a promise?"

"Absolutely. I will be polite, courteous, deferent…"

"Hmm."

"Really, I will, George, and not just for you. For Gabby." Josh was sincere, although he understood why George was concerned. A weekend at a musty old stately home was not Josh's idea of fun, but when George had come back from his art therapy session raving about Gabby's plans to reinvigorate Merton Hall—the Bowes family residence for more than four hundred years—Josh knew it was the perfect anniversary gift and called Gabby right away to reserve a room. She'd been delighted to accept his booking and had emailed him several times since to confirm they were still coming, dropping cryptic clues about the evening's entertainment being 'more to his liking', but he didn't care about that, only that George enjoyed himself.

The satnav directed Josh to take the next right turn, which was an even narrower road with no markings and traversed increasingly dense woodland, plunging them into pitch-darkness. He switched the headlamps to full beam, grateful for their imminent ETA. Sure enough, less than a minute later, they reached the entrance to Merton Hall.

The gates opened as they approached, and Josh drove through them, slowing to the designated five miles an hour, which gave them a chance to be wowed by the change in scenery as they glided smoothly along what could only be described as an avenue lined with willows, their delicate weeping limbs illuminated by small, white lights. With the fluttering snow, the view was truly enchanting, and it seemed an age before the hall itself appeared, tall but not foreboding, bedecked as it was in understated festive décor.

Illuminated evergreen garlands adorned the ground-floor windowsills and the swooping banisters of the steps up to the entrance. To the right stood a conical tree, around thirty feet in height, while to the left were several parked cars with their noses to the house.

Josh pulled his car into the space alongside the closest—a mud-splattered Range Rover—and switched off the engine. Unclipping his seat belt, he turned so he could see George, who was staring up at the building. Josh watched him, at once mesmerised by the way his eyes glistened, ever reminiscent of the finest emeralds twinkling beneath the feathery shadows of his lashes. Indeed, Josh was so enthralled he missed the smile forming, and by the time he noticed, it had become a fully fledged grin.

George pointed up. "It's a castle."

"Pardon?"

"It's a castle," George repeated, but Josh had heard perfectly. He, too, leaned forward and peered up through the windscreen.

"So it is." The top of the building terminated in crenellations. It had been too dark to see them from afar, and up close they were ancient—fifteenth-century, Josh estimated—and impressive. Or they would have been if he wasn't so disconcerted. He'd misread George's reaction—something that hardly ever happened—and his delight was not for Josh's attentiveness but for Merton Hall's architecture.

Without further delay, and in an effort to shake off his discomfort, envy, disappointment—whichever of those it was, potentially all three and more—Josh tugged the key from the ignition and opened the door.

"We should go in before—" A blast of dry-ice wind blew the door back against his shin and took any remaining words and his breath away. He swore in his head and decided it was probably for the best. He was being ridiculous. He tried again, succeeding in getting out of the car, and forged his way to the rear. They'd avoided the worst of the weather on the drive here, but now the snow was coming down in heavy sideways drifts and fought his efforts to lift the boot hatch.

George arrived just as Josh managed to hoist it open and held it up whilst Josh lifted their case out. The boot slammed shut as soon as George released it.

"Man, that's some wind!"

Josh grunted. The magic was dwindling rapidly and the weather had lost its appeal. He clicked the key to lock the car and leaned down for their case, but George beat him to it, giving him a quick smile as they moved off together towards the enormous front doors.

"What's up?"

"Hmm?" Josh frowned. He'd hoped George wouldn't notice.

"You've gone quiet."

"Have I?"

"Come on, Joshua. Talk to me."

He sighed. "It's fine. I'm fine. Just momentary silliness. I thought you were grinning at me."

"I *was* grinning at you."

"Because of those..." Josh tilted his face up to indicate the battlements and immediately wished he hadn't. He blinked away the wet snowflake that had blown into his eye and muttered, "This weather."

"Yeah," George agreed vaguely. Josh gave him a querying look and smiled, dipping his head bashfully. The grin this time was all for him. "Thank you," George said.

"Why are you thanking me?"

"For this weekend. I know you're doing it for me."

"Not *all* for you," Josh argued. He paused as they climbed the steep stone steps to the double, black-painted doors, clearly designed to admit giants, and pressed the bell button. "It's almost as if the Bowes designed their programme especially for us."

"Almost..." George said, inviting interrogation, but it would have to wait.

Chapter Two

THE DOORKNOB—ONE OF two, both big as tenpin bowling balls—turned, and the left-hand door opened, creak-free but with no haste. Josh and George took a step back for no real reason other than everything was so huge it seemed too close—or everything other than the man before them. He was Josh's height, though slightly broader, and completely dwarfed by the glittering cavern behind him. In black tie and morning coat, pale-grey vest, white wing-collar shirt and grey pinstripe trousers, he had to be the Bowes' butler.

"Good evening, sirs," he greeted with a genial smile. "The Sandison-Morleys, I presume?"

"Good evening, and yes, we are," Josh confirmed.

"Please, do come in." The butler swept his arm in welcome. From nowhere, a younger man, in similar attire minus the jacket, scurried forward, squirrel-like, virtually snatched the case from George's hand and scurried away.

George and Josh exchanged bemused glances but did as the butler bade and stepped through the portal…into another world.

The experience wasn't entirely new to them; they'd visited stately homes on school trips where they'd felt like naughty little boys trespassing—*do not touch the exhibits, do not sit on the furniture, do not pass beyond the rope*—hardly daring to look around for fear that it, too, was prohibited. This time was different; they were invited guests, not quite past feeling like trespassers, but the status carried with it implicit permission to touch what they liked, sit where they wanted and look at everything. And there was not a rope in sight.

"You're the first of our guests to arrive," the butler informed them as he took their coats and, with the ease of extensive practice, neatly deposited them on hangers attached to a rail to the left of the doors. "We're expecting two more this evening, the rest tomorrow."

Josh and George nodded dumbly, trying to take it all in as they followed the butler through the hall, which wasn't as bright as it had first seemed. The high ceilings gave the lights little hope of fully illuminating the space, and not for lack of lumens: two chandeliers, at least a dozen wall sconces, plus a small lamp on each of five low, round tables positioned to the side of a staircase the width of a double-decker bus. Against the opposite wall were six large, brown leather sofas, arranged in three sets of two facing each other, and still with room to spare.

On they went, through a wood-panelled screen door, beyond which the hallway continued several yards further before it terminated at a lift with a black iron concertina gate.

"Are you both physically able?" the butler asked.

They nodded to confirm they were.

Bypassing the lift, they came to another set of stairs, slightly narrower than the first, and ascended two short flights, the second doubling back on the first. A quick glance upwards confirmed the staircase completed a further two twists of the helix, but they stepped off at the first floor and followed the spritely butler down an echoey corridor carpeted richly along its centre, paintings at haphazard intervals between the closed doors on either side. With all the wood panelling, the house's construction had to have felled an entire forest.

"And here we are." The butler came to a halt and grandly swung open a door, poking his head into the room before he permitted Josh and George to enter. Both did so, silent but for the squeak of a floorboard or two, determined to keep their thoughts to themselves until the butler had gone. Their case had beaten them there and rested on the dark oak ottoman at the foot of the bed.

"I'll send someone to unpack for you—unless you'd prefer—"

"We'll do it ourselves," Josh interrupted, adding a quick, more gracious, "Thank you."

"As you wish, sir. You'll find your information pack on the dresser, along with the details to connect to our virtual itinerary."

"Sounds like we're in for a busy weekend," Josh muttered, not intending for his remark to be heard by anyone, but other than the bed and a Queen Anne chair in the corner, the room had a lot of bare surfaces to bounce sounds back, so both the other men heard every word.

"On the contrary," the butler said amenably. "Her Ladyship—Lady Gabrielle Porter, that is—requests your presence at supper this evening, but she wants to be clear it is a request and, if you would rather, I will arrange for supper to be brought to you wherever you should choose to spend your evening. Tomorrow, after breakfast, there is a guided tour, optional for all guests, and in the afternoon," on this point, he addressed George only, "the art workshop will take place in the west wing studio—"

"Are you ready to go back to school?" Josh whispered, making sure only George heard him this time. George slow-blinked but otherwise kept his attention fully on the butler.

"—during which, I believe, sir," he addressed Josh, "Her Ladyship has arranged access to Merton Hall's library for you—again, only if you wish it. There is no obligation for you to partake in any of the weekend's activities, though I should add that Her Ladyship is of the opinion you will enjoy tomorrow evening's entertainment."

There it was again—the hint of an evening designed with Josh in mind. He wasn't sure he wanted to know; the possibilities were too horrifying. *A jester? Do they still have those?*

"Sunday's schedule is less frenetic, but I'll leave you to read it for yourselves. Do you have any further questions, sirs?"

Or a performance of The Mousetrap? *Please not a séance—* A sharp nudge from George broke Josh out of his imaginings. "Hmm?"

"Any questions?" George repeated, and Josh shook his head. "No, thank you," George answered on both their behalf. "You've been very helpful."

With a bow, the butler back-stepped and was almost out of the door when George stopped him. "What do we call you?"

"I'm so sorry. I anticipated Her Ladyship would have informed you. How remiss of me." He stepped forward again. "Cosgrove, sir."

"Mr. Cosgrove..."

"Just Cosgrove," he corrected but accepted George's handshake. "If there's anything else you require, there is a phone on the dresser. This also works." He reached up and jiggled the rope dangling from a small brass bell that hung to the right of the door.

"Got it, thanks," George said, after which the man actually made it out of the door and quietly closed it behind him. At last, they were alone and could properly explore what would be their quarters for the next two days.

"Well, isn't this something!" Josh remarked with undisguised delight as he moved around the side of the enormous four-poster bed draped in deep-burgundy velvet. He followed the curtains up to the canopy overhead—an outrageous carved edifice with what could only be described as gargoyles at each corner.

George moved closer to examine the carved head closest to him and grimaced. "Looks like...an owl with a man's face. It's lucky neither of us suffer from night terrors."

"I'd posit these gargoyles are intended to be apotropaic," Josh said knowledgeably.

"Say what?"

"They deflect evil rather than typifying it."

"Ah. Yep. I think I'd run a mile if I came face-to-face with one of these things." George stared at the ugly carving a little longer and then rotated on the spot to take in everything else. The window was hidden behind floor-to-ceiling curtains in the same deep-burgundy velvet as the drapes around the four-poster; the heavily embroidered, swirly-legged Queen Anne chair, ornate oak dresser, wardrobe and ottoman were clearly antique, as was the bed, and no doubt worth a fortune; paintings, not prints, were affixed to every wall. "This is so over the top for a guest room. D'you think they're all like this, or are we getting preferential treatment?"

"Time will tell," Josh said, undecided as to whether he hoped it was the latter. He appreciated Gabby's efforts to make them feel welcome, but at the same time, he didn't want a fuss.

"Hey, come and try this out."

Josh hadn't seen George move, but he was now lying on the bed, or not quite lying, as the pillows were well stuffed and kept him almost upright. He patted the space beside him.

"How is it?"

"Come and see for yourself."

"If I get too comfortable, I won't want to get up again."

George shrugged as if to say *and that's a problem because…?*

With a sigh, Josh relented and sat to take off his shoes. Already, from this action, he was aware of the mattress's snug support around his hips. He shuffled, with difficulty, until he was far enough up the bed to rest back on the pillows and lift his legs.

"Wow. This is incredible."

"Isn't it?" George said. "I'm gonna sleep like a baby."

"Most babies don't actually sleep much."

"Figure of speech, Joshua." George threw off one of the pillows and rolled onto his side, propped up on his elbow, so he was facing Josh. "I'll give Lib a call in a bit, let her know we're here."

"Speaking of babies…" Josh shuffled closer and plucked an escapee downy feather from George's stubble. "She'll be fine."

"Yeah. I mean, she's stayed with my mum and had plenty of sleepovers at Poppy's." George was trying to reason with himself. It wasn't their first night away from her, but it was their first time leaving her home alone.

"Sean's not going anywhere all weekend," Josh reminded him.

"I know." Still, George's worry persisted.

"And everyone else is at most ten minutes away, but we could be home in an hour and a half...weather permitting." Josh really hoped George wouldn't take him up on that.

George smiled. "Thank you, but no way are we going back out in that. Like you say, she'll be fine." He didn't quite believe it but successfully pushed his concerns aside. "So...are we going to accept Gabby's invitation to supper?"

"Do you want to?"

"Do you?"

"I think we should."

"That's not what I asked."

Josh pondered and realised, to his surprise, that he did want to. "Yes," he confirmed. "But if it looks even remotely like I'm going to say something I shouldn't, you need to kick me—really hard."

George chuckled. "OK."

"I'm serious, George. You do know it was my advice that led Gabby to ditch law and become an art therapist, don't you?"

"Yeah, you've both told me, more than once. What's it got to do with this weekend?"

"Her father."

"Right?"

"I hate him."

"Have you even met him?"

"No, but he's the reason she was studying law in the first place. He wouldn't let her study psychology, and she had to actively defy him to do so. He didn't talk to her for the entire three years we were undergraduates."

"Huh. Someone who sulks longer than you do. That's amazing."

"I do not sulk!"

George didn't deign that claim with a reply. "Maybe you'd be best not talking to the man at all?"

"That's precisely my plan, but it might be unavoidable, in which case—"

"Kick you really hard."

"Yes, please." Josh moved to sit up, but George pushed him so he fell back against the pillows again. "George…"

"I checked the itinerary. Supper's not for another hour yet."

"I see. I take it you've already decided what you want to do with…"

George's slow, gentle kiss instantly silenced Josh's chatter, both external and internal, and he moved closer, reciprocating and relaxing into the welcome comfort of the embrace. He wouldn't ever admit it aloud, but he'd been nervous about this weekend. So far, it was living up to his expectations in most respects—the vast, impersonal manor house and equally impersonal staff, a full itinerary prior to Saturday evening's merriment—whatever it turned out to be. His impression, increasingly, was that it had been organised specifically with him in mind, and he was still wondering what Gabby would come up with when, in truth, they hardly knew each other. A lecture on Freud's life?

George had continued to kiss Josh while his thoughts roamed, but now he eased away to study him. "What are you thinking about?"

"Tomorrow night. Sorry. Come back."

George smiled and homed in on Josh's lips again. In spite of his comment that they had an hour until supper, he didn't seem to be taking it any further.

"What are we doing?" Josh asked.

"Kissing," George murmured.

"You don't want to…do anything else?"

"No. I'm good with this. It feels nice. Romantic."

"Romantic, you say… There are four ugly gargoyles watching us."

"Joshua, it's snowing, it's nearly Christmas, and we're spending our anniversary in a castle. Could it be any more romantic?"

Josh had to concede George had a point.

Chapter Three

A S PROMISED, THEY were left alone to reach a decision about supper, and by quarter past eight, they were ready to leave, but they didn't know where they needed to be.

"We could ring the bell," George suggested.

"We could," Josh agreed, but neither moved to do so. It was far too alien a concept. "Let's just phone the butler." He went to the dresser and picked up the phone—discordantly modern in contrast with the rest of the room—handing it to George, who sighed but took it and then stared at it in bemusement.

"There's no instructions. What do I do?"

"Try the hash key," Josh suggested. "At the university, that puts you through to a switchboard. They might have the same kind of setup here."

George did as instructed, and Cosgrove answered. "Hello, Mr. Sandison-Morley. How may I help you?"

"Hi. Um…are you allowed to call me George?"

"If you'd prefer it."

"Yeah, if you wouldn't mind."

"Not at all. How can I help you, George?"

"Please could you direct us to where we need to go for supper?"

"Certainly. I'm about to leave for the evening, but I'll send someone up right away."

And he really did mean 'right away'. No sooner had George put the phone down than there was a knock at the door—the same young man as had taken their case earlier. He didn't say a word as he accompanied them down the stairs and along a passage, delivering them to an open set of double doors and at last a familiar face. Gabby came dashing over and hugged them both warmly.

"It's lovely to have you here! Come in. You know Harriet and Xander, of course…"

Josh didn't, but George had met Gabby's children a couple of times. Harriet was coming up on thirteen and the spitting image of her mother when Josh had first known her. Xander was three years younger and, fortunately for him, looked nothing like Gabby's cousin, whose name he shared and whom Josh had butted heads with in their first year as undergraduates.

"This is Howie, my husband," Gabby introduced.

"Hello," Josh greeted quite formally, but Howie clasped his hand and squeezed rather than shook it.

"Good to meet you," Howie said, repeating the same greeting with George.

"And this is my brother, Andrew," Gabby completed the introductions. Andrew offered a stilted 'hello' and stayed in his seat.

So that was the first surprise at supper: the lack of formality, insofar as they were still seated at a very long dining table that could have comfortably catered for at least twenty more people, but they were all clustered around one end. Nor did servants deliver the food; Gabby and her husband did, and the meal wasn't of the stuffy, formal, quail-eggs-and-roasted-game variety Josh had expected, although he rather thought he'd have preferred that to the rich pasta dish and olive-heavy focaccia they were offered because 'everyone likes pasta'. Still, he was not one to look a gift horse in the mouth, or not on this occasion, given the second surprise of the evening, which only occurred to him after they'd been eating for a while.

"Gabby, why didn't you tell us it would only be your immediate family sharing supper?"

She smiled apologetically. "I thought you would know."

"But this is your parents' home."

"Yes, it is, and we don't live here. However, you won't find them staying for these weekends, despite our father's incessant desire to interfere in everything we do. Mum was quite firm in telling him how it would be—he tasked Andrew and me with finding more innovative means of opening the place to the public, and he should jolly well trust us to do it."

That made Josh smile. He'd never forgotten what Gabby had said about the way her father treated her mother, possibly the way he treated all women, but it sounded like she was fighting back, and good for her. Josh had minimal direct experience of the upper classes, most of it gleaned from his reluctant association with the law students at university, but from what he'd witnessed, and in spite of changes to inheritance laws, patriarchy remained a formidable, unchallenged enemy to equality between men and women in the highest echelons of British society.

Josh didn't interrogate Gabby further, instead observing her family's interactions as supper progressed, posing questions in his mind. How well did Howie treat Gabby? Did he merely 'permit' her to run her art therapy centre or did he actively support her? Did he treat her as an equal? Was he a good father? It seemed that way, assuming he wasn't putting on a performance of 'doting dad and husband' to impress their guests. When the coffee arrived, he poured for everyone, and it was excellent coffee: strong and flavourful but not at all bitter—the kind of coffee Josh would drink all night if he thought he'd get away with it without forgoing sleep.

Meanwhile, Gabby's children, her brother and George tucked into dessert—a very lemony mousse topped with a mountain of cream. They were seated such that Andrew was at the head of the table, which had irked Josh until Gabby explained they'd tossed a coin to decide who *didn't* have to sit there as they both hated it. Gabby sat to Andrew's right, then Josh and George, with Harriet, Xander and Howie on the opposite side of the table.

"Shall we go somewhere a little more comfortable?" Gabby suggested once those who'd opted for dessert were finished.

She'd asked the question generally but maintained eye contact with Josh. Much as he didn't want to decide on everyone's behalf, it appeared he had no choice, so he gave the coward's answer.

"I don't mind."

"He does," George said.

Josh glared at him, and George shrugged, a sneaky smile passing between him and Gabby. They were scheming, and Josh didn't like it one bit. However, his plan to tackle George came to nought when they relocated—not to a stuffy drawing room, as Josh had been anticipating, but to the east wing's solarium, which would presently have been a stellarium were it not for the murky blue-black sky. Snow was falling in fits and starts, accumulating in arcs along the bottoms of the panes in the full glass dome above and lending to the oddness of the room's interior: several mismatched sofas, a drinks cabinet, computer, telescope and an inordinate number of houseplants. It also felt as if it should have been cold and draughty, yet it was almost too warm.

With a sip from the brandy glass Gabby placed in his hand, Josh was instantly drowsy, or perhaps just relaxed. He sometimes found it impossible to tell one from the other. Either way, he settled next to George on one of the sofas and half-listened to the discussion taking place between Howie and the children.

"Daddy, may we take the dogs out now?" Harriet asked while her brother unconvincingly endeavoured to look bored by the whole affair.

"Not tonight, sweetheart."

Gabby leaned down to Josh's ear to murmur, "My father has lurchers—wilful beasts, they are. Smelly, too."

"But you said we could," Harriet protested.

"The children adore them, of course," Gabby added.

"That was before it started snowing. It's too cold now—"

"We'll put coats on."

"And late, Harriet. Let's leave it for the morning, shall we?"

"But, Daddy—"

"No, that's enough."

Harriet stomped away, putting as much distance between herself and her father as was possible in a round room that was sizeable but not big enough for a near-teenager to go off in a huff. Howie sat heavily on the sofa opposite Josh and George's and shook his head.

"It *is* cold," Gabby agreed supportively. She propped on the arm of the sofa next to Howie, who took her free hand, lacing their fingers together.

"I did promise," he said, sounding disappointed.

"Well, then, you're only postponing your promise a few hours."

Howie smiled up at her, and Josh melted a little deeper into the sofa, happy to be proved wrong about their 'arranged' marriage. They were clearly very much in love. Gabby met his gaze, and an understanding passed between them—another stark revelation to join those he'd had since they reunited a year ago and he'd acknowledged how significantly he'd underestimated her friendship.

As undergrads, they'd been too shy to be more than classmates driven by the same desire, nay, desperate need, to excel. They'd had some very deep conversations, during which each had confided to the other things they'd told no-one else. Yet, it was only now that Josh realised Gabby had cared about his future happiness as much as he'd cared about hers, and both were pleased by what they saw.

"So a day of art tomorrow, then..." he remarked to get the conversation flowing again, and not because of Gabby's scrutiny. He was fighting a yawn and feeling brave enough to ask what else she'd planned.

"For the artists," she confirmed. "Did Cosgrove tell you I've reserved the library for you?"

"He did, yes. Reserved?"

"It's yours exclusively for the day—out of bounds to everyone else."

"That's..." Overwhelming.

"It's a beautiful library, with so many rare volumes. Lots of first editions."

Josh had a sense for how George felt when he became tongue-tied, and he really needed to tell Gabby how much he appreciated the opportunity, but the possibilities were exploding in his mind. A private library filled with books he most likely had never seen before nor would ever see again; a day was hardly enough, but he'd take what he could get.

"I think what he means is thank you," George said, squeezing Josh's hand until he winced.

"Yes!" he squeaked. "Thank you."

"You're most welcome," Gabby said, laughing. "And then, in the evening…" She paused to look behind her at Andrew, who had been fiddling with the telescope the entire time they'd been up there, but apparently he'd been listening too.

"A murder mystery," he said proudly.

"Oh!" That was the third and, thankfully, last surprise of the evening, not including how lovely Gabby's family were and how much Josh and George were enjoying their company. "Murder mystery?"

"Yes," Andrew confirmed with an ear-to-ear smile. "The hall has a long and intriguing history. Lots of people have died here over the centuries. We commissioned the creative writing class at my university to come up with murder mystery scenarios inspired by those deaths."

"That's a clever idea," Josh praised, which—astonishingly—widened Andrew's smile but earned Josh a cool look from both Gabby and George. It *was* clever, if not a little macabre. Josh took another small sip of his cognac, feeling quite intoxicated. "Did you say *your* university?"

"Yes. I'm a professor of history."

"Oh, are you? I wasn't aware of that."

"You're an academic too, Gabby told me."

"Sort of. I did lecture for a while, but I'm actually a psychotherapist."

"And a forensic profiler," Andrew added.

"Erm…yes," Josh confirmed, aware of Gabby shrinking, such as she could when she was sitting on the arm of a sofa. He smiled to reassure her he didn't mind that she'd told her brother about his professional life; equally, he hadn't been aware she knew so much about it, and he was a little perturbed the information had come from her art therapy sessions with George, which put them on ethically shaky ground.

"How's Sean doing?" Gabby asked. "I haven't seen him for a while. We really must arrange lunch again soon."

"Oh, he's fine," Josh answered. The question, as far as everyone else present was concerned, was mere small talk, but Gabby had followed his train of thought and nipped it in the bud by confirming Sean was her informant, not George, and once again impressing Josh with her analytical prowess.

It would, undoubtedly, have served her as well in a legal career as it did in her therapeutic calling, but he remembered their conversations as undergraduates—how her father had planned to put her to work managing the estate, and how inadequate she considered herself to be in comparison to the other law undergrads. Her talents would have gone to waste and she'd have been miserable, never reaching her full potential, and for the first time in the twenty-three years they had been acquainted, Josh was confident his advice to her had not only come from a place of compassion, but it had also been sound. He would, of course, be revisiting that conclusion once he was a little less inebriated by fine brandy and excellent company.

The rest of the evening passed very pleasantly indeed. With a little interference from Xander and a fortunate though short-lived break in the clouds, Andrew successfully pointed the telescope at Orion, and the two of them spent a while marking down their scant observations on an old-fashioned star chart. Harriet also recovered from her grumpiness quite quickly—against the yardstick of how long it took Libby to do the same—and came to sit next to her father, who extended an arm around her while

continuing his conversation with George about Farmer Jake's—
the educational farm where George worked.

For all that Josh liked Howie and his everyman presentation,
his evangelising about the importance of British farming was
far removed from the reality of the job that saw George muck-
shovelling for hours every day, whatever the season, and still
came from a place of class and privilege. In the grand scheme
of history, it wasn't so long ago Howie's ancestors had made
a substantial proportion of their fortune from the farmers
who leased their lands, but the man couldn't be faulted for trying,
which was more than could be said for the real lord and lady
of Merton Hall.

"So where are your parents hiding out this weekend?" Josh
asked the next time Gabby looked his way.

"They have a villa in the French Alps—Le Dévoluy."

"Oh, really? I was born not far from Le Dévoluy—well, a
couple of hundred miles away—in Eygalières."

"I think I've been there—it's a little village on a hill, isn't it?"

"That describes most of the villages in the province," Josh
pointed out. "But yes, it is."

"Lots of olive groves, I recall."

"And vine fields."

"Mmm…" Gabby's eyebrows rose briefly in thought.

Knowing his picky eating at supper had been noted and also
exactly what she was going to say, Josh pre-empted. "I'm not a
very convincing Frenchman."

"You speak the language," Gabby countered.

"Poorly." He didn't want to get into a discussion of his
knowledge of French, fearing it would, inevitably, lead to
discussing Xander—Gabby's cousin as opposed to her son—who
was fluent in the language and a show-off to boot. However, Josh's
fear once again proved unfounded as she shifted the conversation
back to the relatively safer territory of their itinerary for the next
two days.

"We're waiting on two more guests this evening—"

Howie interrupted to ask, "Do we know why they haven't arrived yet?"

"Thunderstorms. Their take-off was delayed."

"Anyone I know?" Josh asked cautiously.

"I doubt it. They're journalists—a journalist and a photographer. They're going to run a feature on the hall in *Country Life* magazine. I hope that's all right. Perhaps I should've warned you…"

"We're pretty well used to the intrusion by now." If he sounded blasé, it was because nearly three years of living with the potential for paparazzi to pop out in front of them in the frozen food aisle during their weekly shop had normalised the experience to the point Josh rarely thought about it, although it didn't happen as often as it used to, back when Kris first became a TV celebrity. Knowing Josh was a very private person, their friends had expected him to be affected the most, but after the absolute violation of being a passively consenting participant in a psychological study at university, it was nothing. However, Gabby still looked pensive, so Josh repeated his assurance. "It's fine, really."

"That's a relief. We need all the free publicity we can get." Gabby glanced over at Andrew, who was still poring over his star chart. "Our parents are on the brink of bankruptcy."

Chapter Four

G AB..." ANDREW WARNED, but she dismissed him with a
wave of the hand.

"Josh and George are my friends. It will go no further."

Andrew eyed them both with scepticism.

"You have our word," Josh said.

"What's this?" George asked. Josh gestured for Gabby
to continue.

"There's a strong likelihood the house will have to be sold."

"That's why you're opening it to the public."

"We've always had open days, and they were awful. God
knows what possesses parents to bring their children to a place
like this only to spend the day trudging from room to room
looking at antique chaise longues and paintings by artists they've
never heard of. Almost anything has to be more interesting."

"Did you have ropes?" Josh asked, a touch facetiously. Gabby's
laughter burst from her in a bubble of glee.

"As a matter of fact, we did. Thick, gold ropes, like Rapunzel's
hair. If we were home from school, we'd be confined here with
Nanny for much of the summer, and she was wonderful, but
there's only so long one can keep small children occupied." Gabby
smiled fondly in reminiscence. "She's coming here tomorrow, to
lend us her support."

"She'll be proud of us," Andrew said.

"I do believe she will."

There had to be a tacit comparison underlying their
interchange. Without context, it seemed such a strange thing
for adults to say—highly successful adults at that—but they
didn't elaborate.

The moment hung in the air, with both seemingly caught up in their thoughts until Gabby next spoke. "We're fully booked, but we'll still only make enough to pay the staff for the next month. There are less extreme options than selling or declaring bankruptcy. We could sell some of the land to developers, for instance—most of the larger estates have sold off all but the few acres of grounds immediately surrounding the house.

"We have thirty square miles of forest to the north that has been neglected since the eighties, and the last few farmers with long-term tenancies retired years before that. Their houses are ruins and the fields lie fallow. There really is little point to keeping hold of land we can't manage, and our father won't entertain Andrew's or my ideas—or he hasn't until now.

"If we can prove to him that we can make a success of the public openings doing them *our* way, perhaps he'll be more willing to listen."

Josh nodded his understanding. He had nothing to say, or nothing that would help Gabby. She had a successful career, had married well and produced an heir, yet her father was still dictating her decisions. Then again, Josh had always had a great deal of freedom—more than most of his peers—so it was difficult for him to understand why anyone kowtowed to a domineering parent. From what Gabby was saying, she wasn't going to inherit much in the way of wealth, although even in cynical modern times, the status meant something.

The evening was still quite young, but Josh could convincingly contend the combination of the drive, supper and cognac had him exhausted. The truth was more along the lines of struggling to contain his opinions. He faked a yawn and gave George a light nudge with his elbow. George frowned at him.

"Are you ready for bed?"

"Getting that way. We can stay if you want."

"No, it's OK." George sat forward, ready to stand. "We haven't got an early start tomorrow, have we?"

Gabby shrugged. "The kitchen will serve breakfast whatever time you rise, so if you want to have a lie-in and give the tour a miss—"

"Oh, no—that's not why I asked. I'd like to come with you guys when you walk the dogs."

"Are you sure about that?" Howie said, and Gabby and Josh both laughed at his wide-eyed disbelief. George's puzzlement didn't improve things.

"Unless you don't want me to."

"No, come with us!" Xander said quickly.

"Yes!" Harriet said. "That's OK, isn't it, Daddy? If George comes with us."

Howie was still perplexed why George would want to, but he said, "Fine by me. Assuming our journalist guests arrive soon, we'll head out…I don't know. Around nine? Or is that too early, George?"

"Not for me." Seeing as George was out of the house by five-thirty when he was working early shifts, it was a slovenly lie-in.

"Excellent." Howie unwound his arm from around Harriet and rose from the sofa. "I'll call housekeeping, get someone to accompany you back to your room."

"That won't be necessary," Josh said. "I'm sure we can find our way."

Howie wasn't convinced and looked to Gabby for guidance. She nodded her approval. "All right, then." Howie took Josh's empty glass from him and shook his hand, then George's. Gabby was up on her feet too and began to extend her hand to Josh, then dropped it, then extended it again. A blush bloomed on her pale cheeks, almost instantly spreading up under her glasses and down to her neck.

Josh grimaced on her behalf, all the while aware of his own cheeks burning. How two mental health professionals with more than thirty years' experience between them could still be so awkward around each other, he didn't know. Well, he did, but he preferred not to consciously acknowledge it. She was George's art therapist, after all. If George wasn't confiding in her, they were doing it wrong.

Ultimately, they both decided to just go for it, and as the last of the space between them diminished, they met, not in a swift, polite embrace and back pat, but a prolonged, tender hug.

"Thank you for coming, Josh," Gabby murmured into his neck. "It means a lot to me."

"Thank you for having us," Josh replied in the same fashion.

Releasing each other with a smile that was perhaps a little less self-conscious for the cognac, they made plans to meet after breakfast, and Josh and George departed, leaving the Bowes-Porter family to the rest of their evening.

Ten minutes later, Josh was cursing his complacence.

"It was definitely the first floor," he said, his patience wearing thin as George set off up the stairs to what was surely the second floor, except these were not the stairs they'd come up with Cosgrove when they first arrived. Nor were they the main stairs the servant had taken them down when they went to supper.

"I remember that painting," George said, striding ahead.

"I don't," Josh muttered and increased his pace to catch up. Another bend in the corridor brought them to yet another set of stairs. "For God's sake. How many does one house need?"

George rolled his eyes and gripped Josh's hand. "Come on. It's along here."

"You sound very sure of that."

"That's because I am, Joshua. Those are the stairs we came up, so it has to be this way."

Josh grunted. He was generally quite good at finding his way, but Merton Hall was a maze of corridors and stairs, and more stairs, and more corridors, all of them so similar as to be almost identical.

"This is us," George said, quite smugly. But then, Josh supposed, as the key twisted and the door swung open on their room, he had every right to be.

"How on earth did you do that?"

"The paintings."

Josh flopped into the Queen Anne chair. "I think I might join you for the tour tomorrow."

"Ah, see, I knew you loved those visits to stately homes really," George teased.

"Hey, I've only ever been to three—four now—but I'll never find my way around this place on my own."

"Three?"

"Harewood House, Blenheim Palace and Castle Howard."

"I remember going to Harewood House in primary school." George took off his shirt and hung it in the wardrobe. "That was the trip where Dan got suspended, wasn't it?"

"Yes, it was," Josh confirmed. He sometimes forgot how much of an idiot Dan had been when he was younger. Had he stayed that way, they'd never have become friends, but these days, he was serious and sensible, perhaps overly so. Still a lunatic.

"I wonder how much that vase was worth," George mused and continued talking with his back turned as he took off his shoes and unfastened his trousers. "It's not like they were gonna miss it, were they? They had hundreds of the things. No way did anyone still live there. It was like being in a museum…I guess it was one, really. It feels different here, though, doesn't it?" Now only in his T-shirt and boxers, he turned around. "What?"

Josh shook his head, struck dumb by the sheer power of physical attraction. Like a storm surge, it was as unpredictable and unexpected as it had always been. He'd imagined, in the long years before they came clean and admitted they were in love with each other, that the impact would lessen if they were together, but it had not. The only difference now was he didn't have to hide it, and on rare occasions, when he caught George staring back at him, he knew beyond doubt the attraction was mutual.

"Are you going to sleep in your clothes?" George asked. His eyes twinkled in that way they had of exposing his desire—so obvious now Josh couldn't believe he'd been oblivious for so long.

"Joshua?"

"Yes, sorry." He fought his way out of the chair—it was surprisingly comfortable if not a little musty-smelling—and commenced battle with his shirt buttons. "Aren't you cold?" he asked. The house wasn't well insulated, and the draught coming under the door and sneaking past the heavy curtains was brutal, even with clothes on.

"A bit," George admitted. He stepped into Josh's space, locking eyes with him as he reached down and unfastened his bottom shirt button.

"I can manage," Josh protested, though it was less than heartfelt when George's mouth was closing in on his, and a downright lie once their lips met. "Get into bed," he whispered into the kiss.

"Not without you."

"You just don't want to suffer cold sheets on your own."

George grinned. "You know me far too well."

Chapter Five

J OSH JOLTED AWAKE, heart hammering, and at first assumed it had been a dream, forgotten but for his fear response, always the same in sleep; he froze—a sensible impulse, given he couldn't have outrun a new-to-walking one-year-old—which also gave him time to process the unfamiliar sensations before he was fully cognisant.

This castle is bloody cold. Castle...at what point did I decide it was a castle?

Still hoping he could drift off again, though experience told him it was futile and this was him awake now, whenever 'now' was, he called to mind the stark, formidable silhouette of Merton Hall's battlements that had met them on arrival. He knew nothing about the place beyond it being Gabby's family's historical home—embellished by what Andrew had told them last night—but battles must have been waged there, and those battles would be documented in the house's library. With any luck. Conventional British historical records were, after all, the product of a victorious empire, not factual accounts, and the current aristocracy was a self-claimed endangered species whose members did their very best to stay out of the limelight, afraid that raising their heads above the parapet would get them metaphorically decapitated in this land of restless peasants whose ire burbled on a stove constantly tended so it never quite reached boiling point. The last thing the landed gentry needed was the 'The Common Man' to know how often they had faced extinction.

So it had been for centuries, Josh had learned at school. His knowledge of English history was good; he'd go so far as to say it was very good. He'd studied it to A' Level and had, several times, almost changed his mind and applied to study history instead of psychology at university. Had he mentioned that to Gabby? He didn't think so, although his love of books and research was enduring and not a secret. He'd relish a day in any library. A day with Merton Hall's library all to himself? Heaven.

His strategy was working, and he was on the cusp of sleep when he was once again startled to wakefulness. Definitely not a dream this time, but a loud cracking sound followed by the whisper of cloth brushing against something else. And it was close by, in their room. Someone was in their room.

As if stirring in his sleep, Josh rolled onto his back and let his head fall to the side so he was facing the direction from which the noise had come. He opened his eyes a fraction. *There, over by the window.* He discerned movement, a dark figure with back turned, and reached out across the mattress for George to tell him they had an intruder. He didn't find him.

"George?"

George jerked in surprise and turned with palm instinctively clasped to his chest.

"Sorry."

"It's OK. Did I wake you?"

"No. At least, I don't think so." Josh threw back the covers and got out of bed. He made it three steps before he backtracked for the duvet, pulling it tight around him as he joined George at the window. "Why are you awake?"

George nodded, directing Josh's attention to the view outside. The window was facing its own siege, fending off the large, wet snowflakes impacting and sliding down to join several inches of accumulation on the frames around the many square panes and on the broad sill below.

"Brr—" Josh gasped, mid-shiver, at the flash of fork lightning that touched down in the near distance, followed immediately by another loud crack, this time identifiable as thunder, although it sounded different to any thunder he'd heard before. "Wow! I've never seen snow and an electrical storm at the same time."

"I have," George said. "Thundersnow."

"Did you just make that up?"

"Nope." George continued to gaze out the window, utterly entranced, and Josh could see why. It was a sight that had inspired legends; beyond the swirling blizzard was a starless, eternal void but for momentary glimpses of vast, ragged-edged clouds, stretched across the sky like the limbs of angry gods reaching for Earth.

"You might want to reconsider that dog walk in the morning," Josh advised.

"The storm'll pass by then." George shifted his eyes Josh's way. "You're cold."

"Freezing."

George put an arm around him—and the duvet—and drew him close, huffing hot breath down his neck. Josh sighed. It was warming him up nicely. "This *is* very romantic," he admitted. "What time is it?"

"About five, I think."

That was later than Josh had anticipated. "I might as well shower and dress. There's no point in me going back to bed." He tried to move, but George squeezed, tightening the circle of his arms. "I thought you might want the duvet."

"I'm wide awake."

"OK. Then...I'll just stay here."

"Good." George kissed his head and pressed their cheeks together. Lightning flooded their field of vision, briefly dazzling them, but no thunder this time. The snowfall seemed to have slowed slightly too, which was for the best; as the storm dissipated and morning light gradually spread upwards from the east—to their right—it revealed a winter wonderland, the only break in the white-out courtesy of the underside of the larger trees and sheltered corners of the low walls marking off areas of the hall's extensive grounds.

It was beautiful, and romantic, and Josh wished they could stay right where they were forever, except his feet felt like they'd been encapsulated in ice. Reluctantly, he withdrew from George's embrace, ditched the duvet and snatched up his dressing gown as he dashed for the bathroom, soon after also ditching his plan to take a quick shower, lured by the antique bathtub, a stunning piece with ornate cross-top taps, black iron claw feet and deep, deep sides. He stuck in the plug and turned the hot tap fully on. A high-speed gush of water was quickly joined by a cloud of steam that promised he wouldn't be cold for much longer.

**

George took the itinerary from the dresser over to the bed and lay on top of the duvet, his ears tuned to Josh's progress in the bathroom. Josh very rarely used the bath at home for lots of reasons, but these days it was mostly because he had no patience for languishing. George loved a good soak, as did Libby, and he hadn't anticipated having to fight for one this weekend. He skimmed down the day's programme; there was time enough for a bath, if he still wanted one, between the afternoon's art workshop and dinner.

It promised to be a great weekend—the kind he'd only dreamed of until three years ago, when all their time apart and the pretence of being OK with never being more than friends was wiped out in one fell swoop by Josh's admission. He'd been in love with George all along, which made for a lot of catching up whilst trying not to dwell on what they'd missed.

Josh hadn't been lying to himself or anyone else; he just hadn't realised it was love. None of their friends got it—how he could've been so blind to his feelings when he was so clued in to everyone else's—but George did. Or he did now. Josh could switch his feelings on and off at will, blocking out anything he found overwhelming or didn't understand.

He'd be doing it in the bath, focusing his thoughts elsewhere to distract from the sting of hot water against his wrists and other less comfortable sensations that caused him to relive what he'd done. He also knew to completely avoid anything that triggered those feelings when he was sick, or relied on George to intervene, just as George relied on him. Josh's brain worked differently from his, which switched off completely when he couldn't deal with something. Maybe that was what had drawn them to each other when they were young. They picked up on each other's screwy wiring…

Next thing George knew, Josh was standing a few feet away from him. George groaned and sat up. "So much for being wide awake. How long have I been asleep?"

Josh pulled his phone from his trouser pocket to check the time; apart from wet hair, he was ready for the day. "Not long. I was only in the bath half an hour. Forty minutes, maybe?"

"Guess I was more tired than I realised. What's the weather doing?" From where he was, he could only see the grey-white of the sky and the occasional snowflake fluttering by. Josh went back into the bathroom, leaving George to answer his own question. He went and peered out the window.

Josh returned, brushing his hair. "How bad is it?"

"Not very. Three or four inches, at a guess," George dismissed. He'd seen some serious snow on the ranch, although not so much in December as in the spring. Typically, the year they'd all come to visit him for Thanksgiving, they were hit by a major storm, and the airport was closed, along with most of the local roads, until the deluge stopped and the ploughs could make headway through the several feet of snow.

"You would say that," Josh muttered, clearly on the same wavelength. "Are you still going dog-walking?"

"Yep. Shower and breakfast first, though." He kissed Josh on his way around the bed, calling back as he stepped inside the very steamy bathroom, "D'you think they'll mind if we turn up early?"

"I think we could do exactly as we pleased and no-one would bat an eyelid."

George frowned and shut the door, pondering that statement as he stripped off. It did seem like everything about this weekend was geared around their interests, or what Gabby believed their interests to be. Art and libraries were obvious, but a murder mystery…well, George knew how she'd come up with that idea and hoped Josh hadn't figured it out, as unlikely as that may be. He set the shower running and stepped under the mighty downpour, then leapt out again, drenched and with no idea whether it was really hot or really cold. Leaving it a few seconds, he cautiously tested with his hand, and swore.

Too hot. Way too hot, and he couldn't reach the dial to turn it down without scalding his entire arm in the process. He looked around the bathroom for something he could use to bash the dial from a safe distance—a soggy loofah, Josh's shampoo, a bottle of shower gel, their toothbrushes—in other words, nothing of any use. He went back out to their room.

"That was quick," Josh said, watching him through the mirror, his eyes widening at George's nude streak.

"Not done yet. I can't turn the shower down."

Josh switched off the hairdryer and went to look. "Ah, I see. I can probably reach that." He unbuttoned his shirt cuff and started rolling his sleeve up. George came tearing over to intercept, standing between Josh and the shower cubicle.

"Hey, just because you can't feel how hot it is doesn't mean it won't scald you."

With a smirk, Josh looked him up and down. "It's difficult to take you seriously when you're stark, boll—"

"Joshua…"

"For goodness' sake. I'm not going to just stick my arm in there. Look." Josh whipped the hand towel from the rail, dropped it into the sink and turned the cold tap on full. Then, wrapping the drenched towel around his arm first, he reached into the shower and gave the dial a quick turn to the left before extracting his arm and dumping the towel into the bath. "See? Not a scald in sight!" he boasted, waving his arm in front of George's face. George caught it and looked Josh in the eye.

"You're telling me it didn't even hurt a tiny bit?"

"Not even a tiny bit." Josh's smug tone might've fooled most people, but it didn't fool George. "I'll leave you to shower," he said, casting one last sultry glance over George's nakedness on his way out the door. It was an invitation to take it further, but if Josh had been interested in doing so, he wouldn't have dressed in such a hurry.

George didn't pursue him and instead finally got around to taking his somewhat more temperate shower but decided to leave shaving for later, figuring he was an artist and could get away with looking a little unkempt. He was also ravenous, not helped by having been awake half the night—a weird state of affairs. He could count on one finger the number of times he'd lain awake while Josh slept, and soundly; the storm had been rolling back and forth for a good hour before it woke him.

"Did you know they're running one of these weekends every two months?" Josh looked up from his phone screen as George emerged from the bathroom.

"Are they?"

"According to their website." He shook his hair back from his eyes. It immediately flopped forward, and he tried again. "Must be the water," he said.

George nodded noncommittally and gathered his clothes whilst Josh continued to fiddle with his phone, interspersed with exasperated huffs. The next time George looked his way, he'd scooped his hair back and was keeping hold of it. It was ultra-fine and sensitive to static, so maybe the storm was to blame rather than the water, although it got on his nerves more days than it didn't. Still he wouldn't entertain the idea of wearing it in a shorter style or anything remotely different to how it had been since…forever. George was glad about that. Josh's hair was one of the many things he loved about him. If he ever did the unthinkable and let Shaunna loose on it with a pair of scissors,

George wouldn't get to torment him anymore about how it always looked the same whatever he did with it, but he honestly didn't care if Josh went completely bald—other than he'd miss the smell of his shampoo.

"OK. That's saved to my phone now," Josh said, switching hands and scrolling. "So, breakfast…imminently, I would think. I can smell food cooking."

George sniffed. "Is that bacon?" The mere possibility had him almost tripping over his jeans in his haste to get them on.

"From a rare wild boar, no doubt."

George chuckled but didn't comment. Listening to Josh's scathing criticisms of their hosts in private was preferable to having him go head-to-head with them in front of an audience and the press. "What time's the tour again?"

"Eleven—I'm going to join you for that."

"Um, OK." He'd thought Josh was joking when he'd said it last night.

"I want to see the battlements."

"In this weather?"

"When else will I get the chance?"

"We could always come back."

Josh gave him a doleful look.

George shrugged. "Just an idea. Can we go and find breakfast? I could eat a horse."

"Hmm." Josh grabbed his jacket from the wardrobe. "Don't say that in front of Gabby, or you'll be having *médaillon de cheval* for dinner this evening."

Chapter Six

"GOOD MORNING, MESSRS. Sandison-Morley," Cosgrove greeted them as they descended the stairs to the entrance hall.

"Good morning, Cosgrove. How are you?" Belatedly, George realised it probably wasn't the done thing to ask after a butler's well-being.

"I am well, thank you," he replied out of courtesy. "Breakfast will be served in the morning room. If you would come with me…"

Cosgrove waited long enough to ensure they were following and then led the way past the dining room where they'd eaten the previous evening, along a corridor which, aside from the paintings, looked identical to all the other corridors they'd walked up and down. They turned a corner and entered a large conservatory furnished with small tables and chairs, all brand-new, most likely bought to accommodate Merton Hall's guests on this and future weekends.

"I'll let the kitchen staff know you're ready for breakfast," Cosgrove said, herding them to a table next to the steam-obscured windows, not that they needed a clear view; the blurry whiteness was so bright it hurt.

Once he was satisfied they were settled, Cosgrove marched off, at speed, returning less than a minute later with two more people—a man and a woman, whom he delivered to the table next to George and Josh's, with the same spiel about breakfast, adding, "Ms. Coltrane and Mr. Shapiro are from *Country Life* magazine. Messrs. Sandison-Morley are personal friends of Lady Gabrielle Porter."

The four exchanged quick, quiet hellos—just enough to satisfy Cosgrove—before he departed once more. A few moments of slightly awkward silence ensued, during which the woman sized them up. George sensed Josh getting tetchy and was about to intervene, but the woman got there first.

"Clara Coltrane." She half rose from her chair to shake their hands. The small bag strapped diagonally across her chest slid and knocked with a heavy thud against the table. She tugged the strap, and the bag whizzed under her arm and disappeared behind her back. All the while, she kept her thickly made-up eyes on them, or on Josh mostly. "And you are...?"

"Josh." He said it as if she were tearing some great secret from him under threat of death. George understood why when she turned her piercing gaze on him.

"George," he obediently provided.

"Good to meet you both. And this is my photographer—"

"Matt," the guy finished, no handshake. He was a lot younger than Clara, more casually dressed, and didn't even take his hands out of his jeans pockets or look their way, instead staring upwards, which prompted George to do the same. Apart from the snow covering the entire glass roof, there was nothing to see. "Guess I'm just shooting the interior," he muttered.

"Whatever you think," Clara said through a fake smile on a par to the ones George's mum shot at Josh when he was accidentally sarcastic. With everyone else, his sarcasm was quite deliberate.

So, erm..." Clara frowned at Josh, seeming to search her memory for his name but giving up. "You're a friend of erm..."

"Gabby, yes," Josh confirmed.

"Right, and are you, erm, a, erm..." She cleared her throat. "Are you here for the weekend thing?"

"Artist? No. Here for the activity weekend, yes."

"Hmm-hmm." Clara nodded for far too long. "How do you, erm, know...erm..."

"Gabby?" Josh offered with a puzzled frown as if he was unsure himself. George felt the dreaded tickle of giggles in the back of his nose and switched to staring at his lap. He didn't really find Clara's struggle for words funny. He knew firsthand how stressful that could be, although she didn't seem overly bothered. Nor did she appear to have noticed the delay in Josh's response. He, too, was on the brink of giggles, and when he finally spoke, his voice came out tight and reedy.

"Gabby and I were at university together."

"Is that recently?"

"No. We graduated over twenty years ago."

"I'd love for you to tell me more." She sat forward, and her bag reappeared in her lap, from which she plucked an audio recorder. Setting it on the table, she went back to staring at Josh. He pointedly considered the recorder for half a minute or more before he gave a nonchalant shrug. George admired his cool façade. Josh would be calling her all sorts of very uncomplimentary names in his head.

"There isn't much to tell. We studied psychology together. She went on to train as an art therapist. I trained as a psychotherapist. We lost touch until last year—"

"So you weren't always friends?"

"We weren't always *in touch*," Josh said evasively, and if he was completely truthful, they weren't really in touch now. Obviously, they'd communicated to arrange this weekend; before that, they hadn't properly spoken since George went for his first art therapy consultation—in spite of both telling him, several times, how much they regretted not staying in contact.

"George, is it?"

He nodded. No point pretending otherwise.

"You're the artist in the family?"

"I guess you could say that. I sketch and paint a little."

"What do you think of the art here at Merton Hall?"

"I haven't had a chance to look at it properly yet, but from what I've seen, there're some excellent paintings." George knew what he liked and what he didn't, and he'd choose the classic landscapes over abstract weirdness any day, but he'd left what little he'd known about art history behind when he passed his A' Level.

"And such a fascinating past…" Clara cocked her head to one side, watching him and waiting for his thoughts.

He shrugged. "I'll have to take your word for it. I've never been here before. I don't know anything about the place." Josh might, but if he'd shared, George hadn't been listening.

"Well, I'm sure we'll learn all about it during today's tour."

George had nothing to say to that and didn't dare look at Josh because Clara's tone was patronising, and if George had noticed, Josh certainly would have. As it was, two women in blacks and whites arrived with a silver trolley—their breakfast—which they unloaded onto the two occupied tables: pots of coffee and tea, jugs of milk and four plates with silver covers.

One of those plates arrived in front of George, and the waitress or whatever she was lifted the cover away, revealing a very ordinary-looking Full English, thankfully. George had been expecting eggs Benedict or smoked salmon or some other posh concoction. He didn't mind food like that, but it was too much first thing in the morning and in any case didn't fill him up.

Once the wait staff had departed—no thanks forthcoming from Clara and Matt—George tucked in, still keeping his head down other than when an extra sausage and egg landed on his plate. He briefly looked Josh's way, but Josh kept his eyes on his breakfast. Beneath the table, his leg jigged up and down, yet his expression remained passive. He was angry and containing it.

The journalist's attitude had got to George too, even though he should be used to it by now—working-class kid, moved to a middle-class school, made middle-class friends, somehow got into university—he didn't really fit in and had been subjected to snobbish value judgements all of his life. He knew who he was and where he came from, and while he wasn't proud of his background—it just *was*—nor was he ashamed. What he'd achieved in his life was down to his mum's sacrifices, so he could get a decent education, and to Josh, who had always believed in him, encouraging him to try harder at school, to stay on and take his A' Levels, go to university.

George was well aware how fortunate he was and what his life would've been like without their support, but he was still a working-class man. Outside of the estate where he grew up, almost everyone he met was of a higher social status, including Cosgrove the butler. But that didn't make them or this journalist better than him, just luckier with their lot.

Mostly, he didn't care. He kept to himself, tried to get along with everyone, and his friends accepted him. That was what mattered. The rest of the world could go to hell.

Even so, he got a bit of a kick out of subtly watching Clara suffer her crappy breakfast. She had gritty stuff, quinoa or bulgar wheat—it was hard to tell—which could be tasty if it was cooked creatively, but she was hating every mouthful whilst trying really hard to look like she was enjoying it. George knew because he'd seen the same expression on Josh's face when he was pretending he liked something George had cooked for him. For that reason, he'd given up on introducing Josh to a varied diet...until Libby came into their lives and figured she'd have a try. It was pretty much the only time Josh complied without complaint, and George loved him for it.

Clara suffered her breakfast for as long as it took Matt to clear his plate, after which the two of them slurped coffee and noisily clanged cups against saucers whilst they discussed how they'd go about their day. It was a tedious conversation that sounded more like bragging than getting organised, but George wouldn't have to endure it for much longer; he could hear signs of life elsewhere in the house and eagerly watched the door, almost leaping out of his seat in joy when Harriet appeared, grinning broadly.

"Good morning, George. Are you still coming to walk the dogs with us? Cosgrove said he'll find you some boots if you are."

Matt clapped his hands. "Dogs, of course! I knew I recognised you!" He swivelled to face George. "You're friends with Kris."

"I, um…"

"Kristian Johansson? The actor?"

"Yeah, I knew who you meant." George wasn't impressed by the guy's attitude, never mind being recognised yet again, all because a trashy magazine had published photos of him and Kris walking the dogs.

"Who?" Clara asked.

"The guy who played the lead in *Shadows*?"

"*Shadows*… Wasn't that one of those…erm…" She clicked her fingers, attempting to recall.

"Scandinavian crime drama."

"Right… Oh! *Him*! He was much better on the radio. He's not hot property anymore, is he?"

"Depends who you ask," Matt replied, giving George a smile that made his skin crawl. He'd heard enough and was desperate to leave, but there was no telling what would happen if he left Josh with those two. Well, he could imagine all too vividly, and it wouldn't be pretty. If they were anything like the hacks who had hounded Kris, it could cause irreparable damage to Gabby's reputation.

"Are you ready?" George asked, prepared to drag Josh away by the scruff if need be. Josh was breathing hard out of his nose and his eyes were blazing, but he gave a single, sharp nod and got up, his fists clenched to his sides as he stormed ahead of George, past Harriet and along the corridor, only stopping when he reached the hall.

"They're an absolute fu—" he began, but even in his fury had the decency to modify his language in front of Harriet. "Awful people," he finished.

"Yep." George couldn't agree more. "You need to keep away from them."

"Don't you worry. I have no intention of engaging them."

"And if they engage you?"

"No comment."

"Josh…"

"No, that's what I'll say. No comment. Whatever they ask me—no comment."

"OK." George had a feeling Josh's strategy would fall at the first hurdle, but maybe they could avoid each other. It was a big house, after all. "So are you gonna come with us?"

"No. I think I'll see what Gabby's up to."

"Mum's setting up her studio for this afternoon," Harriet said.

"Ah. Well, in that case, I might go and find the library."

"She won't mind you joining her."

"I'd hate to be in her way. And I really don't mind…" Josh trailed off at Cosgrove's arrival. He was carrying two pairs of black boots.

"Thank you," Harriet said. "But we only need some for George."

Cosgrove nodded in acknowledgement and held out one pair to George. "These should be the right size. If they're not, do let me know."

"Thanks." George took the boots, his curiosity getting the better of him. "Do you have a cupboard full of boots in all sizes?"

Cosgrove smiled reservedly. "Not quite, but we keep a few pairs here for regular guests—rest assured, we clean them inside and out after they've been worn."

"Fair enough." George wasn't worried about wearing someone else's boots. It wasn't like he'd be putting his bare feet in them.

"Do you require anything else. A hat? Gloves?"

"No, I've got those, thanks." At this time of year, he kept them in his coat pockets.

"Is there anything else I can do for you?"

"Yes," Harriet said. "Please will you take Josh up to the art studio?"

"Of course, Miss Porter."

George once again had to stifle his laughter. Josh was flabbergasted, but Harriet was as astute as her mum, and Josh hadn't done well at hiding his disappointment when she'd told him Gabby was busy. Whether it was the shock or an atypical instance of Josh *not* cutting off his nose to spite his face, he didn't protest Harriet's suggestion.

"We should go, George," she said.

He nodded and turned to Josh. "OK?"

"Yes. Go and have fun."

"You too." With some reluctance, George departed with Harriet to meet the others.

"Don't worry," Harriet said, blithely striding ahead. "Cosgrove won't let him get into trouble." She reached a door in the wall in front of them and waited for him to catch up. "Better brace yourself. Grandfather's dogs are boisterous."

Chapter Seven

"OH, GOD. THAT'S a long way down." Josh backed away from the panoramic windows fronting Gabby's third-floor studio.

She laughed, but not at him, he didn't think, and came to stand by his side. "You do realise you were this far up last night?"

"Ah, but I couldn't see that, could I?"

"That makes a difference?"

"It did last night." It wouldn't now he knew. "So the solarium is in the east wing?"

"Correct. At the top of the other turret."

"You have turrets?"

"We used to. The house was rebuilt in 1661 and again in 1863, after the east turret fell off."

Josh gulped audibly.

"It's all right," Gabby comforted. "Architecturally, they're towers now and go all the way to the ground."

"Just as long as *we* don't," Josh muttered, although it wasn't so bad if he stayed back from the windows, and the view was absolutely stunning. "Has this always been a studio?"

"Since the late 1700s, yes, but not in my lifetime—until now."

"But—" Josh clamped his teeth together. He'd promised to behave himself this weekend.

"I'm an artist?" Gabby guessed. Josh nodded mutely. She sighed. "Let me finish up, I'll order some coffee and then we'll talk." She quickly typed into her phone and continued with what she'd been doing when he arrived: setting easels in a semicircle in front of the windows.

"Can I help?"

"Hmm…bring those over?" She pointed to a stack of Perspex paint palettes in the centre of the floor. Josh collected them and left one on each of the stools Gabby had placed in front of the easels.

"I'm sorry if I said the wrong thing," Josh said, glancing up from what he was doing.

"You didn't say anything."

"I was going to."

"Yes, and you're right to question it, but there are things I've never told you about why my parents were so insistent I study law, or, should I say, were so against me becoming an artist."

"Art therapy and creative art are entirely different animals," Josh argued. Quite why he thought he needed to when he was talking to an art therapist…well, he didn't need to.

"Indeed they are, and I do believe my father finally understands the distinction. But you know how it is. Superstition can override reason in the best of us."

Josh didn't agree; he wasn't in the least superstitious, but he held his tongue, aware that such a statement was also a value judgement of Gabby's admission, and he wanted neither to offend her nor jeopardise his chances of hearing what was sure to be a story full of the kind of intrigue he loved, as opposed to the awful pantomime this evening's murder mystery would prove to be.

Cosgrove arrived with a tray, which he set down on the low windowsill for want of anywhere else for it to go, accepted thanks with his usual cool grace, and departed. It was at that point Josh noticed the cushions covering the rest of the wide ledge, which Gabby perched upon, leaning back against the glass. Josh's stomach made a lurch for his mouth.

"Come and sit," Gabby invited, patting the cushion next to her.

"God, no. I'll sit on the floor," he said and did exactly that.

"I had no idea your phobia was so pronounced." Gabby was notably astounded but passed his coffee down to him rather than attempt any kind of desensitisation, for which he was eminently grateful. Most people, qualified or not, tried to fix him or persistently reminded him he was in no real danger, as was true on this occasion, but phobias weren't rational, and no amount of spouting physics at him could make them so. He supposed, if he were to be generous, the same was true of superstitions. Now, if he could just hold onto that thought whilst Gabby shared hers…

"This room…" she said, wistfully looking around her and prompting Josh to do the same.

Ironically, other than the conservatory, which was almost entirely made of glass, the studio was the only space Josh had been in that wasn't covered in paintings. The ceiling and curved wall connecting the tower to the rest of the house were matte-white; the floor was bare stone over which a few shaggy rugs were strewn, including the deep-blue one upon which he was sitting.

"What? It's cursed? Haunted?" Josh asked. He wasn't being facetious. "Rapunzel's former prison?" And now he was.

Gabby laughed. "Funny you should say that. Remind me later, I must show you something."

She'd piqued Josh's curiosity, as had everything he'd seen and heard so far. He set it on a mental back burner and waited for Gabby to continue with what she'd been telling him.

Eventually, she smiled ruefully. "If I said yes, it's cursed, would you mock me?"

"No. I'd ask why you think it."

"And if I told you every artist who painted in this room died before their time?"

"I'd ask what the hell you were thinking inviting my husband to paint here." Josh broke out of their hypothetical dialogue to say, "If you really believed it was cursed, you wouldn't be holding the workshop."

"That's very true," Gabby admitted with a certain amount of relief. "My grandmother—my father's mother—ended her life in this room."

"Met the end of her life or actively brought it to one?"

"Hard to say. I don't remember her well, but I recall she was incredibly eccentric, dancing around in bare feet and always singing. My mother recently told me she once caught my grandmother sniffing the white spirit she used to clean her brushes, and I realised she wasn't eccentric, she was high. Her cause of death was recorded as lung disease, unspecified."

"That would fit with inhaling white spirit," Josh concurred.

"She was the eleventh of my ancestors to die in here, all of them artists. My grandfather locked and boarded up the door and strictly forbade entry. After he died and my father took over the estate, he considered transforming it into a hotel and moving us to the gatehouse, which—" Gabby turned and squinted out the window "—you can just about see from here."

Between listening to Gabby's tale and his increasingly numb bottom, Josh's curiosity gave him a sudden spurt of daring. He rose to his knees and crawled to the windowsill, looking where Gabby pointed. "Wow, that's quite a size."

"Yes. It has six bedrooms—more than the east wing, which was our living quarters and is still my parents'. We really should've moved. We'd have been comfortable there."

"Why didn't you?"

"Because my father changed his mind when he reopened this room and found his mother's paintings. My grandfather had stacked them against the walls and left her easel where it was."

"Let me guess, with an unfinished painting on it?"

Gabby smiled. "That would've been rather fitting, but no. There was no unfinished painting. The thing is, Merton Hall has always been too big for our family, and I know you're probably thinking that's true of all stately homes, but we're quite impoverished compared to our peers, and every penny is spent on the upkeep of this blasted house and its staff.

"I said last night my father won't consider selling some of the land. It's because he wants to sell the lot, get rid of it once and for all. His father felt the same, and there were others before them, but every time anyone came close to selling, something happened to stop them."

"If your parents are on the verge of bankruptcy, surely they have no choice but to sell," Josh reasoned.

"Unless history repeats itself and they're saved just before the stool's kicked away. That's why I've never wholly dismissed the notion of a curse—maybe not on this room, per se…"

"Sounds more of a blessing."

"It would be if we could let the place go to ruin, but it's a World Heritage site, so we're stuck with it until such point as the Fates permit us to part with it. Oh, look!" Gabby pointed. "There's George."

Cautiously, Josh twisted and peered down, miraculously holding on to his breakfast as he watched the small band of dark figures, almost indistinguishable at this distance when all were in hats, coats and Wellington boots.

"Where are the dogs?"

"Miles away, I should imagine." Gabby sheltered her eyes from the blinding sky to peer into the distance. "Yes, they're right over there."

Josh decided against looking up and continued to watch George, Howie and the children. They were having a snowball fight, and it seemed George was under heavy attack. He'd be having the time of his life.

"Well, I'm afraid I need to go and get ready to receive the rest of our guests," Gabby said, sounding more regretful than apologetic. "I'd much rather spend the time with a dear friend." She took his hand in hers and held it for a moment. "Thank you for listening without judging."

"Oh, I was still judging," Josh said with a grin.

Gabby laughed. "Then thank you for not voicing it. Are you still coming on the tour this morning?"

"After you've spent the past half an hour tantalising me? I can't wait!"

"Excellent. Now, you're welcome to stay here—"

"No, no. I'll come down with you," Josh said hastily.

They both stood, and Gabby straightened the cushions and gave the room a cursory glance over. "And you say you don't believe in superstitions…"

"I don't. However, I do believe in very great heights." As if to illustrate the point, Josh came over dizzy and staggered—a little more dramatically than was warranted. "Also, I'll get lost." He gestured with a sweep of the hand. "After you, Lady Gabrielle."

She narrowed her eyes at him. "Please don't call me that. It sounds so…condescending."

"I meant it as a joke." Which was in poor taste when she'd been privy to his anti-aristocracy rants at university.

"In that case, my apologies for being over-sensitive," she dismissed and headed for the door.

"Gabby."

She stopped but kept her back to him.

"I'm sorry. I didn't think about…well, you know how I feel, and…" He sighed and gave up trying to explain. "I just want you to know I respect you tremendously."

She turned his way, smiling. "You've never learned, have you?"

"Tact and diplomacy?" Josh shook his head. "Sean gave it his best shot, but I'm a lost cause. Although I did successfully avoid telling your journalists to…eff off."

"Oh, they're dreadful people. I suppose they have a job to do, like the rest of us, but…well, thank you for not telling them to… eff off." She repeated Josh's words, pause and all, and they both laughed briefly, but it quickly petered out. Gabby had more to say. "For the record, I respect you tremendously too."

Josh blushed, past pretending her opinion didn't matter to him and once again feeling terribly exposed.

"Come on. Let's go before this gets awkward."

"Good idea." Josh followed her through the door, casting one last look at the room—a blank canvas awaiting its next story, hopefully not as tragic as those that had gone before.

***

"I got him right in the face!" Harriet squealed and dived behind George, resulting in him taking the full brunt of the snowball Xander hurled back at his sister.

"Ow!" George rubbed his arm while Xander cackled like a crazy thing and compressed more snow between his small yet strong hands. "I hope you're preparing more ammunition down there." George glanced behind him where Harriet had stockpiled half a dozen snowballs already. "But you probably shouldn't aim for your brother's face. You could hurt him." Luckily, Harriet's snowballs were much less compact than Xander's.

"When we've won, can we build a snowman?" she asked breathlessly and continued rolling what would've been her seventh snowball until it was clear she was building a snowman, regardless of how George answered.

"I'm not sure we've got time." It was ten o'clock already, and George was freezing, but he was also having a lot of fun.

"Just a little one, George. Please?"

It was so hard to say no. "Look, your dad's coming over. Let's see what he says, shall we?"

Harriet optimistically carried on.

"George." Howie finally reached him. "The dogs have gone walkabout, and Gabby will have a fit if I leave them out in this weather. Would you mind taking the children back inside for me?"

"Not at all. Or I can go after the dogs if that's easier?"

"Easier for me," Howie said with a smile. "I can't possibly impose."

"I don't mind. I'm pretty good with dogs."

"Awww, are you building a snowman?" Xander tried to run, but he was quite small and kind of zigzagged through the snow. "Can I help?"

"If you want," Harriet answered indifferently but let him join her in pushing the by-now foot-wide ball of snow.

"It's a funny age she's at," Howie mused. "One day she's screeching in fury because we won't let her go to the cinema with her friends, the next she's just a little girl again."

George smiled, watching the two siblings work side by side in harmony. They'd been really well behaved all morning, but he got what Howie was saying about Harriet. Libby was almost fifteen when she came to live with them, but she still had moments like that. "So am I on kid or dog duty?"

"Whichever you'd rather, George."

"Um..." He was torn. On the one hand, he was enjoying spending time with Harriet and Xander; on the other, he'd seen how little notice the four lurchers took of Howie. "I'll go get the dogs," he said.

"I can't thank you enough," Howie gushed as George set off in the direction the dogs had gone. He should have taken that as a warning; four wayward lurchers—a breed known for speed and endurance—soft snow, and as he moved away from the shelter afforded by the house, the wind bit at his face. He tugged his scarf up over his nose and mouth and tightened the draw string around his hood. He had his work cut out.

Chapter Eight

A T QUARTER TO eleven, Josh gave up pacing their room and went downstairs to see why George hadn't come back. He slowed as he neared the entrance hall, whence came the buzz of conversation, the voices too many for him to pick out a single speaker. Bracing, he picked up speed and entered the throng of guests, looking past them in search of George, ideally, but Gabby or Howie would do. Cosgrove caught sight of him and held his position, smiling as amenably as ever.

"Is everything all right, Mr. Sandison-Morley?"

"Erm…you might be better placed to answer that. I'm looking for George."

"Ah, yes. Your husband isn't back yet."

"Why isn't he back yet?"

"He went to fetch His Lordship's dogs, I believe."

Josh sighed in resignation. "Yes, that's something he would do." He noticed Howie arrive and was briefly optimistic, but no. He was with Gabby, not George. They spotted him and came over.

"Good morning, Josh," Howie greeted, fleetingly making eye contact before looking around the crowded space. "Gosh, it seems many more than sixty people."

"Wow, that is a lot," Josh said.

"Yes, Andrew tells me 1891 was the last time every room was occupied."

"What's the significance?"

"Gabby's great-grandparents' wedding, I believe," Howie answered, distracted by the rowdy rabble. "No George?"

"Not yet. How long have you been back?"

"Half an hour. I do hope he isn't lost."

"Is that a possibility?" Josh's alarmed tone bought him Howie's undivided attention.

"Sorry. No, I wouldn't have thought so, but if he isn't back in the next fifteen minutes, I'll ask the groundskeeper to go out in the four-by-four. I'd wager the dogs have made it to the forest. He'll have a hell of a time getting them out of there and a long walk back."

As Howie finished speaking, a murmur spread through the guests. It was snowing again.

Just bloody perfect. Josh's alarm cranked up to the level of minor panic. Finding unfamiliar dogs in thirty square miles of overgrown forest in a blizzard: that was going to put even George's expert-level animal-whispering to the test.

"All right, everyone," Gabby enunciated above the hubbub. "If I may have your attention…" She waited for the noise to die down. "First of all, welcome to Merton Hall. I'm Gabby Porter, or Lady Gabrielle Porter, if you prefer, and over there is my brother, Andrew." Everyone looked where she pointed. Andrew raised his hand in a small, self-conscious wave. "Merton Hall is our family home and has been so since the year 1600…"

Josh tuned out, his attention drifting to the picture window at the far end of the hall and the superb view of the rose gardens it would have offered in summer—not so in winter, and in heavy snow, which was to say it would make a beautiful Christmas card, but it was doing nothing for him. A quick peruse of the Met Office and BBC websites that he'd hoped would calm his frayed nerves escalated his panic from minor to moderate with their talk of 'up to eight inches by nightfall'. *What was Howie thinking, leaving George to fend for himself in this weather?* The consolation *at least there's no thunder and lightning* half formed, and Josh shoved it aside, refusing to attend to it lest he tempt fate…and he'd claimed not to believe in such nonsense.

But it wasn't nonsense to worry that George had lost his way, and as soon as Gabby had finished her address, Josh would demand that the groundskeeper leave immediately. *Demand.*

Like he had any right to boss nobles around, and in any case George had only been gone for half an hour. He was out with Blue for double that every day, rain, shine or snow—maybe not so much snow, purely for the reason Blue didn't like it. Pity the same couldn't be said for Lord Bowes' dogs, but there really was no reason to panic yet.

Alas, after an hour of stumbling along behind Gabby's group, during which Josh had hardly heard a word she said, there was still no sign of George or the dogs. Presumably, Howie had, as promised, dispatched the groundskeeper, and if Josh could've joined the search, he'd have done so, but he'd heard several guests remark that they'd had to leave their cars near the gates because a tree had fallen across the drive. There was nothing for it but to continue with the tour and await news.

It was awful. He felt so utterly helpless. The tour dragged on through corridors and paintings and rooms and vases and chairs and tables and why the hell did they need all this priceless rubbish anyway? With each minute that ticked past, Josh's petulance grew until he could take it no more. He stealthily departed from the group and returned to the staircase, descending at speed to the entrance hall.

"Any news, Cosgrove?"

"No, sir. Not yet."

"How far is it to the forest?" Josh marched over to the rail from which their coats hung; he'd barely made contact with his jacket when Cosgrove intercepted and practically slapped his hand away. Josh eyed the butler in wonder and annoyance. The man was everywhere at once.

"Sir—"

"Josh. Please call me Josh."

"Josh, I don't think it would be wise for you to go after George. The groundskeeper already has two vehicles out searching for him."

Josh went for his coat again, but Cosgrove pushed it further along the rail. Short of shoving the man aside, Josh couldn't reach it. "I can't stay here and do nothing. It's just not in my nature."

"And I can't stop you from leaving, but perhaps you will allow me to distract you a while longer?" Cosgrove's tone beseeched agreement, and the interlude gave Josh pause for more rational consideration. With a heavy sigh, which served to vent some of his tension, he relented.

"What do you have in mind?"

***

The forest was a beautiful, untamed mess guarded by a line of overgrown conifers, beyond those thick-trunked deciduous trees; George wasn't up on the different species, but a few acorn shells littered the ground, so there were oaks in there, and he thought he spotted a red squirrel, although some grey squirrels were reddish-brown. Either way, the forest was teeming with wildlife.

That was how George had located the dogs: the deer were frantic, but the lurchers weren't interested in them. Rabbits and other small creatures, many of whom should have been sleeping the day away or in deep hibernation, ran for their lives, pursued by the silent, dark-grey shadows that streaked between the trees, the only sounds the light pounding of swift feet and excited panting.

George watched and listened, enthralled and with little chance of luring the dogs away from the activity for which they were bred. It would have helped if they'd had even the most basic obedience training, and he was pretty sure, had he known their names, they wouldn't have responded to them anyway. All he could do was wait until they wore themselves out and decided they'd rather be home in the warm than tearing around in wet snow.

The temperature was dropping; George felt it in the cold damp air that sneaked inside his hood, chilling his ears. If he kept moving, he stayed warm, so he set off again, trudging up to the spring that marked the forest boundary at one end, then back down the slight incline to the splintered spruce. The forest extended far beyond that point, but he was using it to mark his location, and now he knew what had made the loud cracking noise that had woken him. One side of the tree's trunk was sheared to ground level, as if it had been spliced from top to bottom by a giant, blunt axe, exposing pale wood and a very strong pine smell that gave George Christmas-morning butterflies but also made his eyes water. He turned and set off back up the hill. It was a test of endurance—his versus the lurchers'—and so far, they were level pegging.

He was halfway back to the spring when there was a kerfuffle a few yards in front of him. A creature squealed and George grimaced, but whatever it was must have gone to ground as the next moment, there was an explosion of powdery snow, and two of the dogs burst from the trees out into the open. They both stopped and had a good shake, then set off at a trot—in the opposite direction to the house.

"You dopey mutts," George muttered and went after them, tugging at the cord fastening his hood. He couldn't whistle with the scarf in front of his mouth, and he couldn't untie the cord without taking off his gloves. He shouted, but the snow absorbed the sound, and the dogs had reached the spring. Any second, they'd round the edge of the forest and be out of sight. Still fighting to untie the cord, George increased his pace to a jog, glad his traversing back and forth had trampled a path through the snow. He'd dropped a glove, but he'd worry about that later, once he'd caught up with those damn dogs.

At last, the cord came undone, and George yanked his scarf down, giving a shrill whistle as he reached the end of the tree line. Panting, he stopped and bent over, hands on thighs, giving his burning muscles a chance to recover and catching his breath. His job kept him reasonably fit, but running through snow was hard.

Preparing for the worst, and expecting the dogs to be dots in the distance, George straightened up. "Ah." He chuckled. "Hunting's thirsty work, huh?"

The other two must have come out at this end of the forest as all four dogs stood, with bums in the air, lapping at the spring.

George let them drink a little longer before he said, "Come on. Let's go home," and, wonder of wonders, all four dogs obediently joined him for the three-mile trek back to the house.

Chapter Nine

THE GRANDFATHER CLOCK'S singular chime nearly gave Josh a heart attack and would have startled him off his feet had he not already been sitting. Indeed, he'd been sitting for almost two hours, on one of the lumpy and not especially comfortable sofas in the hall, but he'd yet to find the motivation to move.

He wouldn't have minded, but Cosgrove had warned him about the clock when he'd left not ten minutes prior to oversee the lunch arrangements. The man was a godsend, one of those everyday psychologists Josh hadn't been aware existed before he allowed George into his life and met Iris Morley. Granted, it made a mockery of his long years of study and the fancy pieces of paper with which he was endowed, but what the likes of George's mum and Cosgrove the butler understood about the human condition wasn't taught in the classroom. It was gleaned from life experience, and it afforded them an expertise Josh could only aspire to possess.

In George's continued absence, Cosgrove had brought newspaper clippings for Josh to peruse and regaled him with stories about the Bowes family, to whom he'd been in service for thirty-five years. None of what he'd shared breached confidence; it was all public record and almost exclusively centred on Gabby, Andrew and their cousin Xander, who had lived at Merton Hall during his early teens.

That had been a revelation, and Cosgrove evidently assumed, as a close friend of Gabby *and* Xander, Josh knew more than he did, which was already far more than he wanted to, so he'd switched to asking banal questions about the newspaper articles, grateful for any and all distractions...as long as they didn't involve talking about Xander Etherington-Bowes.

Most of the clippings were from the local paper, detailing open days past and celebrating insubstantial acts of benevolence on the part of the lord and lady of the manor—a donation to the parish church to re-glaze the sanctuary window, expensive bric-a-brac put up for charity auction. The tone of the locals was muted, neutral, apathetic really. If Merton Hall were demolished tomorrow, a few might lament nostalgically over a rose-hued past and the 'death of British culture', but none would grieve for it, nor for Lord and Lady Bowes.

As for gaining any insight into the earl incumbent and his good lady wife, in the midst of the black-and-white newspaper articles was a feature from *Country Life*, celebrating the Bowes' ruby wedding anniversary and penned by the one and only Clara Coltrane. Josh read the first couple of paragraphs and gave up. He didn't want to hear her smug, nasal whining, real or imagined, but he read enough to determine she had an ongoing relationship with Merton Hall and would report favourably on Gabby and Andrew's *Art of Murder* weekend, irrespective of whether it was the success they hoped for.

Then there was the photo spread accompanying the article— *not* credited to Matt Shapiro—which was flattering, but...who knew if the Bowes were happy and in love? Their gestures were stiff and formal, their expressions caught amid faked toothy laughter as they appeared to casually stroll through the gardens or perched 'cosily' in the drawing room as if it were a space they frequented, yet it had been clear from the moment Josh set foot in Merton Hall that it was a Fabergé egg—an opulent, uninhabited shell barely capable of sustaining life.

It was all rather sad. Here was a family supposedly of status and wealth, yet they possessed neither and instead existed in one drab corner of an immense and, it had to be said, beautiful house, which they'd been trying to offload for a hundred years or more. Their past was mired by tragedy, their present a travesty of sequinned rags, not riches, and cold, empty hearths.

He never thought he'd see the day he'd pity the privileged, and perhaps he was merely projecting guilt for his own. He hadn't asked for it, and he wouldn't willingly give it up, but he felt it in each frivolous purchase and every free choice he made. He had never wanted for anything, nor been forced to take on responsibilities he didn't want, but those were not what set him apart from Gabby and her family.

A silent look of affection and regard when all other eyes are turned coldly away…is a hold, a stay, a comfort, in the deepest affliction, which no wealth could purchase, or power bestow, as Dickens wrote, or, as The Beatles had put it somewhat less poetically, 'Money can't buy me love'. That was what Josh had picked up on and why everyone was so miserable. Merton Hall was a loveless, lonely castle, an unwanted orphan of the past.

"Josh! There you are!"

He'd been so lost in his thoughts, Gabby had essentially appeared from nowhere. She was deceptively small for a grand inquisitor.

"Yes, here I am." He rallied. "How did the tour go?"

"Very well, although a little rushed. For some godforsaken reason, my group wanted to go up on the battlements."

"Why godforsaken? Battlements are fascinating. Did you take them?"

"Fortunately—for me—there's no means to access them anymore. Besides, it would be bitterly cold up there in this—" Gabby pursed her lips, for the most part stifling her gasp as she realised the carelessness of her statement when George was out there somewhere. "You're missing lunch."

"I'm not hungry."

The pause and shift in topic had been swift, less than a second, but it had left its impression on both their psyches, better spoken of than ignored.

"Oh, Josh." Gabby sat next to him. She was so harrowed he wished he'd just suffered lunch, but there was a constriction in his oesophagus like he'd swallowed a lump of lead, and if he tried to eat, he'd vomit. "I'm sorry. You must be terribly worried, but I'm sure George is fine."

"He's been gone for three hours."

"I know, but—"

"Long enough for hypothermia to set in."

"All of our groundskeepers are out searching. They'll find him soon, I'm sure of it."

Josh nodded, trying to accept her assertion or at least appear to, and failing on both counts. "He couldn't have fallen down a well or anything like that?"

Gabby leaned back to peer at him over her glasses. "You do know it's the twenty-first century, don't you?" she teased. He folded his arms and looked away, across the hall. "No," she said. "There are no wells or traps or anything else of that nature. It's a large area to search, but he was well wrapped up…"

Her assurances slid over him and pooled around his feet like so much melted snow. Seeking distraction, he nodded at the large portrait hung not quite in the centre of the wall opposite. "Who's that?"

"Ah, yes! I was going to show you. That's Annabella Moss. A commoner, and a very dear friend of my great-grandmother."

"Was it she who painted it?"

"Yes." Gabby directed his attention to the portrait next to it of a fair-skinned woman whose wide, too-blue eyes and oversized pupils gave her an appearance of perpetual astonishment. "My great-grandmother."

Now he understood how his Rapunzel remark earlier had prompted Gabby's anecdote. Aside from the golden-blonde hair constrained in a long, thick plait winding over her great-grandmother's shoulder, in contrast to Gabby's fine, almost-black hair, the family resemblance was striking—by its absence. Gabby shared not a single feature with the woman in the painting and was still waiting for his verdict.

"She's…beautiful in her own way."

Gabby gave a little *ahem*.

"It wasn't an insult. She *is* beautiful, but she's…unusual-looking." He sighed and muttered, "Shut up, Joshua," which made Gabby giggle.

"She is unusual-looking, you're quite right, and unusual of soul. She almost died of tuberculosis in her early twenties and struck up a lifelong friendship with the woman who nursed her."

"Annabella?" Josh guessed.

"Correct. At the time, my great-grandparents had no children, and the doctor advised it would be dangerous to both mother and baby. My grandfather was born a couple of years later, perfectly healthy, but his birth took its toll on my great-grandmother. I believe Annabella continued to nurse her—if the number of portraits are any measure, she was a regular visitor at Merton Hall, yet no-one ever saw her come or go. Although, according to Xander, she and my great-grandmother were lovers."

Josh contained his scoff to a nostril flare. "It doesn't take a genius to work that out." The portrait of Annabella was all dark reds and pinks behind the sensual swirls of her black hair, framing her soft, flawless complexion.

"Yes, well…it wasn't the painting that told him," Gabby hedged.

Were it not for the ring of the doorbell—as loud as the grandfather clock and twice as shrill—Josh would have broken his promise to behave himself, but hope supplanted all disparaging thoughts, and he bolted from his seat and rushed down the hall, ignoring Cosgrove's disgruntled protestation as he heaved the door open, letting in the weary lurchers who scattered the four directions of the compass.

"Oh, good Lord!" Gabby said. "The floor! Look what they're doing to the floor!"

They could've been doing an Irish jig for all the attention Josh was paying.

"I'll see to it, Your Ladyship," Cosgrove assured her and clicked his fingers to get the dogs' attention—Josh presumed. Right at that moment, he had eyes only for George. The excitable clatter of claws against marble gradually became quieter and then stopped altogether.

George unwound his scarf and exhaled heavily. "It is bloody Baltic out there."

Josh snorted—with laughter and tears of relief, and an almost irrepressible urge to give George a thump for worrying him, but went with throwing his arms around him instead. "What took you so long? You're freezing." He pulled away just enough that he could see George's face. "You realise you almost missed lunch?"

George grinned. "Why d'you think I hurried back? I am *starving*."

"You don't say!" Josh released George so he could unfasten his coat. "You've been gone for three hours, and we missed the tour."

"Why did you miss it?"

"I caught the first hour or so."

"He thought you'd fallen down a well," Gabby tattled.

"A well?" George repeated incredulously.

Josh shrugged. "I don't know what's out there. Three hours, George!"

"Yeah. I've just hiked six miles through the snow. What can I say? It took a while." George looked over Josh's shoulder at Gabby. "I need to talk to you about the forest at some point."

"Oh?"

"It's full of endangered species—trees and animals, maybe red squirrels. They're almost extinct."

"Are they really? That's...useful to know. But even if you're right, we simply don't have the resources to maintain it."

"You could talk to the Forestry Commission or the National Trust or...I don't know. There's got to be some help available."

Josh nodded. "He's right, Gabby. If there are endangered species in there, chances are developers won't get planning permission anyway."

Gabby raised her hands and let them fall with a slap against her thighs. "And there we have it. The perennial fly in the ointment."

"Not necessarily," Josh countered peaceably. "It might attract more visitors. More visitors equals more revenue—"

"Which is exactly what we don't want!" On those words, Gabby stormed off down the corridor towards the east wing—the Bowes' private quarters—making it clear they weren't welcome to follow.

"Whoa!" George stared after her, wringing his woolly hat as if it were soaked right through. "I didn't see that coming."

Josh reached over to still the worried motion. "Sadly, I did."

Chapter Ten

LUNCH, WHEN THEY finally reached it, was delicious. Or Josh thought so. George ate his fill of the poached salmon and sliced potatoes, but his lack of comment or praise for the chef gave away that he was eating out of hunger rather than enjoyment, and that wasn't like him. There again, the food was a bit on the bland side—nary an olive and only a modest sprinkling of the mildest of herbs—thus perfect for Josh's somewhat perfunctory diet, particularly after this morning's large, nasty-tasting dose of his own medicine. It had given him a very clear understanding of why George lost his cool over Josh's penchant for getting caught up in life-threatening drama in the pursuit of answers. No more; he'd promised.

And yet…

Exclusive access to a private library and so much to research—the afternoon couldn't come soon enough. And really, how dangerous could a library be? He supposed he could, perchance, stumble upon a secret passage behind the bookshelves, and if he did—

"Hey, you OK?" George asked. The question, seemingly out of the blue, told Josh he'd been rumbled, but he still played ignorant.

"Erm…yes. Is there a reason I shouldn't be?"

"You kind of slumped."

"Did I?"

"Yeah. Are you worried?"

"Worried? About what?"

"The way Gabby reacted before."

"Oh!" Josh's heart was racing, but not with worry. He was utterly disappointed to realise, after everything, he would still investigate that theoretical secret passage, and there was no chance of him getting away with it, even if he didn't land himself in another life-threatening drama in the pursuit of answers. Irrespective of whether George fathomed what Josh was up to, he'd know he was up to something. *Step away from that passage, Joshua.*

"Are you sure you're all right?"

"Josh, George…" Gabby's call from the other side of the conservatory saved him. He was pleased to see she was all smiles now, no residue of her earlier outburst, and for good reason. At her side was an older woman; it was difficult to put an age to her, but as she and Gabby came closer, Josh noted a familiar air about her—commanding yet compassionate, severe yet kind.

George leaned in and muttered out the side of his mouth, "D'you know who she reminds me of?"

Josh nodded. "Mrs. Kinkade." Their old primary school teacher.

"How did you…?"

"Elementary, my dear Watson."

George groaned, at the Sherlock Holmes reference or the play on words, Josh wasn't sure. However, he was certain of one thing: the presence of her former nanny was having a profound effect on Gabby, so much so she had drawn the attention of quite a few of the other guests, who watched without bothering to disguise they were doing so as Josh and George rose from their seats for their formal introduction.

"Martha, meet Josh and George, very dear friends of mine. Josh, George, this is Martha Perkins, my nanny."

"It's a long time since I was that, dear," Martha dismissed with a chuckle but still beamed proudly as she exchanged handshakes with them.

"It's lovely to meet you," Josh said. "Gabby's talked about you—all good things."

"I'm glad to hear it. And I believe you're the young man responsible for her decision to jettison a career in law."

The stern delivery made it impossible to tell if she was cross or pleased about that. Whichever of those it was, Josh had a feeling honesty was the best policy. If her resemblance to their old primary school teacher were any indication, Martha Perkins would know just by looking at him whether he was telling the truth, and he had no desire to test her patience. Given she'd singlehandedly raised Gabby and Andrew, and quite possibly their cousin Xander too, it had been tested enough.

"Yes," Josh said at last. "It was clear to me from the moment we met that law was the wrong path for her, and I told her so."

"A good job, too." Martha nodded her approval, and Josh quietly vented a sigh. Alas, it took his good intentions with it. He reasoned: he'd been a positive influence on Gabby in the past; ignoring for the time being the part where he threw himself into the single-minded pursuit of answers, why not in the present? Again, he questioned, how dangerous could a library be? The worst that could happen was getting conked on the head by the tumble of a poorly placed tome.

But maybe there was a way around it, a loophole, of sorts, that meant he could still help Gabby and keep his promise to George.

The two women stayed long enough for Martha to thoroughly interrogate Josh and George, to the point she could have hacked their online accounts with the information she gleaned from them, and then it was two o'clock: the scheduled time for the art workshop. With a promise they'd talk more over dinner, Gabby summoned Cosgrove to take care of Martha before she gathered her artists, ready to escort them up to the 'cursed' studio.

"I'll come and collect you when we're done," George said.

"I might be finished before you," Josh argued—pointless obstinacy, and they both knew it.

"Yeah, right."

"Ha! I might just prove you wrong. Before you go, I was thinking…"

George narrowed his eyes. Josh rolled his. "This is about Gabby, isn't it?"

"I have to help her, George. She's my friend."

"I know. But what can we do? It's not like we're in any position to bail her out. Even if we were, she wouldn't want us to."

"And no-one's going to buy Merton Hall as it stands. It needs the upper-class equivalent of the smell of fresh coffee and a lick of paint. I'm going to research the history this afternoon, see if there's anything that might inspire Gabby and Andrew to connect to the place, if only to convince someone else to buy it. But I can't do it on my own—not without it becoming…" Josh trailed off. He was so weak, no willpower. Normal people just did a bit of research, wrote up their notes, moved on.

"An obsession?" George finished for him. Josh blushed. George sighed, a little paternally, and squeezed his hand. "At least you're owning it this time."

"Hmm." Josh doubted it would save him from leaping without looking into the rabbit hole. Or secret passage.

George watched the last of the artists depart. "I need to go, and I've got an idea—I'll tell you later—but yes, let's solve this puzzle together."

"Thank you."

"Be good," George warned and gave him a quick kiss before he jogged to catch up with his temporary classmates.

Josh didn't leave for the library right away, in part because he had only a vague notion where it was and no desire to get lost again. He finished his coffee and listened to the other non-artists; no sign of darling Clara and her sidekick, although George wouldn't have gone so readily if they'd been there. The rest were discussing their plans for the afternoon. The snow had stopped, but the low temperature negated the entire 'weather permitting' section of the itinerary—archery, or 'a short ramble across the estate to Merton Forest' for the nature-lovers. Josh would have laughed at the latter, but his morning of anxiously awaiting George's return had left him a touch delicate.

The alternatives were Merton Hall's games room, wherever and whatever that was—based on what he'd seen so far, it was probably a dusty old barn of a room with a couple of ancient table-tennis tables and carpet boules—or a trip to the local village's artisan Christmas market, which was the vote winner, and they were welcome to it.

Soon after, the main group departed, and Josh was alone once more. Rather than call on Cosgrove to point him in the direction of the library—the man worked far too hard as it was—he waited for the staff to arrive to clear away after lunch. It was the longest five minutes of his life.

***

"…you'll find everything in here—oils, acrylics, watercolours." Gabby patted the front of a massive dark-wood cabinet that followed the curved contour of the wall. "Or chalk and charcoal if you'd prefer. As I said before, there is absolutely no pressure to produce work this afternoon." She acknowledged George, who was loitering near the door whilst she finished giving her instructions. "But whatever you create is yours to take away with you at the end of the weekend. Any questions?"

The artists, all seated, with some already sketching outlines on the canvases before them, remained silent. Gabby smiled permission to those who had not yet begun and then threaded her way between the easels to reach George.

"Everything all right?" she whispered. "Not too exhausted by your excursion, I hope?"

George smiled and shook his head. His quad muscles were aching from working extra hard, but eight-hour days of physical labour and regularly playing football had built up his stamina.

"Can I get you anything?" Gabby asked.

"No, I'm fine, thanks. Where do you want me?" There were two easels not in use at the end of the semicircle closest to the door, one of which had a slightly obstructed view of the landscape, and it was a stunning view: a uniform expanse of white; to the left, a village nestled under the brow of a cottage-dotted hill, and the church steeple pierced the pink-orange glow of the setting sun;

to the right, Merton Forest, or the part of it nearest the house, stood proud and majestic. As if they were aware of their distant audience, crows burst from the treetops in a dark cloud that scattered and spiralled upwards, almost disappearing into the purple gloom as they surveyed their kingdom on the lookout for a new place to settle.

All the while George had been watching the crows, he'd been aware of Gabby watching him. They hadn't known each other for long or spent much time together—six two-hour therapy sessions over the course of a year—but it was intense, concentrated time, not all of it geared towards fixing George's brain. Sometimes they just chatted about nonsense, and they laughed a lot. Gabby was quiet, very calm, and always so patient. Today, he was seeing another side of her—subdued, frustrated, wistful—and it hurt his heart.

"I'm going to…" He gestured to the cabinet, and the two of them went to gather their supplies. George usually worked with watercolours, but they wouldn't do today. He needed the stronger pigments of oils and an excuse to leave his creation behind.

"Have you ever walked in the forest?" he asked as they took up their places at their easels. The quiet murmur of conversations masked his question from all but Gabby, whose continued surprise at his choice of paint delayed her response, but she got around to it eventually.

"When I was young, yes. Many times. Xander and I used to go there together to get some peace—unless there was hunting or shooting going on, which, sadly, was most weekends. I'm opposed to hunting with hounds on the main, but the ban cost us quite dearly in ways that are immeasurable." Gabby laughed ruefully. "Or perhaps not."

George didn't really understand what she was saying. He'd been in the States when the hunting ban came into force in England, and as far as he knew, it was still legal to hunt with dogs in Colorado, but it was nothing like British fox-hunting—red-coated toffs on horseback and a pack of baying hounds. George had seen the damage wild animal attacks caused, and he'd had to shoot them a time or two, but he didn't agree with hunting for sport, which was the kind Gabby was talking about.

"So there's no hunting here at all now?"

"None—"

A knock at the door interrupted Gabby's response, and all heads turned to see who was there. George groaned.

"Hi, don't mind us," Clara said, bustling over. She stopped a few feet behind George and dropped her bag to the floor, audio recorder in hand. "Pretend we're not here."

Easier said than done, with that recorder running and the constant clicks of Matt's camera as he roved around the semicircle.

"As I was saying," Gabby murmured, casting a wary glance at Clara, "we tried drag-hunting for a couple of seasons, but there simply wasn't the interest anymore. In fact, last night was the first time the dining room has been used since the hunt stopped meeting. Go back twenty years, and the house would have bustled with hunters returning to celebrate or commiserate, and they'd stay for supper. Sometimes my parents would host a hunters' ball in the great hall—where this evening's activities will be—and guests would stay overnight.

"Honestly, us children hated the weekends—they were especially overwhelming for Andrew and Xander. So much noise, so many drunk people... Did you live in halls at university, George?"

"Um, sort of. I lived off-campus in a boarding house with about twenty other guys. It was more like a YMCA."

"Did you have parties?"

"Oh yeah." George laughed. The parties were wild—too wild for him to feel comfortable recounting any of the details in front of a journalist.

Gabby took one look at him and started laughing too. "I was going to say...life in our halls of residence was much the same as weekends here in the past, and I couldn't wait to move off-campus.

"But I appreciate now how much we've lost, and I'm not talking about tradition or the social side of hunting. We used to have gamekeepers and livery stables. We even bred horses specifically for hunting, and there were the hounds to care for. Hunting fuelled a small but vibrant industry, and when it was banned, it took all those jobs with it." She paused and held her pencil vertically in front of her, catching a glimpse of George's mostly blank canvas. "Oh, I'm sorry! I'm stopping you from working."

George smiled and carried on slowly sketching his outline. Their conversation had nothing to do with why it was taking him so long, nor did Clara and Matt, although it looked like they were done anyway. A couple of minutes later, they left—more quietly than they'd arrived. Some of the artists seemed disappointed while others were palpably relieved.

Gabby set her pencil on her easel and stood up, addressing the group. "I'm going to pop down and check everything's in place for this evening. Shan't be long."

As soon as she'd gone, George prepared his paint palette. The image was clear in his mind; the tricky part, as always, was transferring it to the canvas, capturing that fleeting moment when the colours and shadows and light were in perfect, magical harmony. If he could achieve that, Gabby might just see the forest as he did.

Chapter Eleven

O LD BOOK SMELL was a drug. Addictive, mind-altering, a lifelong friend who understood his every desire, fulfilled it and more. Josh's mind was simultaneously relaxed and receptive to every sensation, for it was more than the smell of aged ink, paper and leather. Those earth-tone bindings, the gold lettering, the absence of uniformity—he could have spent hours just admiring the spines from afar. But, alas, he had only one afternoon in which to make the most of this magnificent treasure.

Books were time machines, each volume capable of transporting those willing to fully immerse themselves in the written word to times past, present and future, on this and other worlds. A closer perusal of the titles on display spelled out the potential destinations at Josh's disposal—Middle England in the nineteenth century, Middle Earth in the thirty-first, Greece, Rome, the Cotswolds...

From Aesop to Xenophon, Augustus to Vitruvius, Alcott to Wilde—first editions, all of them, and not one in mint condition. Just as it should be.

He could die in this room and know his life had been lived to its fullest. He'd rather not, but he could.

There had to be at least a thousand books, stacked on concave shelves that followed the curve of the west tower's inner wall. He followed those shelves up and across, up and across, until he reached the top shelf just below the picture rail. Several floors above him was the art studio, where George would be creating a masterpiece, though George never saw his work in that light. Josh sometimes wished he could paint; it seemed such a creative way to still the mind, but his love lay here, with the written word.

Storeys and stories; the English language is marvellous.

A gentle rap at the door brought his attention back to his surroundings.

"Will these do?" Cosgrove asked. "They're a little stained by silver polish, I'm afraid."

"Perfectly, thank you."

With a bow, Cosgrove retreated, silently pulling the door shut on his way. Josh had asked if there were any gloves he could wear to protect the books, and Cosgrove had assured him it wasn't necessary. Josh disagreed—as strongly as he could stand to when he was sending the man on yet another mission—so Cosgrove had gone off to find him a pair suitable for the purpose.

Back to the books then. There was some order, a cataloguing system of sorts: Ancient classics and Modern, organised alphabetically by era, origin and author; reference sources— encyclopaediae, dictionaries, thesauri, atlases—Josh recognised the spine of his childhood atlas and couldn't resist revisiting to admire the attention to detail, albeit largely inaccurate in retrospect. He remembered, too, the trouble he'd had switching old country names for new; but then, he'd always struggled with change.

He worked along each shelf, pausing every so often to pull out a volume and cautiously flick through its yellow-edged pages. There was a collection of Ladybird books, mostly classic fairy tales—including *Rapunzel*, he noted—as well as all of Charles Dickens' work, A.A. Milne's and Lewis Carroll's among others. However, the poetry shelves proved the stickiest block to his progress, and he'd read half of *Visions of the Daughters of Albion* before he found the wherewithal to close it and move on, leaving it jutting proud of the rest of Blake's illustrated works so he could come back to it later, if time allowed. That chair by the open fire was begging for his company; the thought of curling up in it with a cup of coffee and a book was enough to spur him on, and he made swift work of locating the volumes that would help him in his quest.

The books about Merton Hall were few in number—only three specifically tackling the hall's history, with several more containing references to it. Thus, there were no shelves fully dedicated to the house, but it certainly paid to have a history scholar in the family; at least, Josh assumed Andrew was responsible for the handwritten index of the entire history section. Judging by the gradual improvement in legibility and style, he'd started at a young age and taken several years to complete his work.

It was only then, with the question half-formed in his mind, that Josh noticed the lack of art books. Law, yes—a shelf full of the things, some of which he recognised from hours spent sitting in Jess's office with nothing to do. He'd read *General Principles of English Law* in its entirety while she'd worked at her desk, pretending he wasn't there.

So no, Gabby hadn't followed suit and indexed the art section because there was no art section. Indeed, aside from the hand-bound *Merton Hall Record of Births, Deaths and Marriages*, which included briefly the cause of death for each of the eleven victims of the 'cursed' art studio, there were no books relating to art at all.

Josh read the death records with interest, particularly the four that included mention of 'suspicious' circumstances, one of which related to Anne Bowes, Gabby's golden-haired great-grandmother. She was found by a maid, on the studio floor and with lacerations to her chest and arms, which could have resulted from self-defence or it could have been a suicide, but the record maker had omitted those details, concerned only with highlighting that the cause wasn't natural.

On reflection, Josh concluded it would have been stranger if the inhabitants of Merton Hall didn't have an aversion to art. However, this small library had comprehensive collections of every other academic discipline bar art...and psychology, which made no sense at all, other than to highlight how small-minded, stubborn and cruel Gabby's father was.

But that was by the by. Josh wasn't doing this for Lord Charles Bowes; he was doing it for Gabby and Andrew. In humans, a sense of belonging was a basic need and, with few exceptions, intrinsic to a sense of well-being. It was enshrined by Edward Coke in English law: 'For a man's house is his castle, *et domus sua cuique est tutissimum refugium*'—and each man's home is his safest refuge. Gabby and Andrew had been denied that, by their upbringing, by the stories that dominated their family narrative, and their disassociation from the family home.

Had Josh believed for one second they really wished to dispose of it, he wouldn't have fought Gabby earlier, and he'd have dissuaded George from giving her the hard sell about the ecological importance of the forest, but that wasn't what he saw. Gabby and Andrew no longer lived at Merton Hall; their only emotional connection to it was via Martha Perkins, their childhood nanny. If they wanted to get rid of it, why had they gone to all the trouble of organising an open weekend and entertaining insufferable journalists to save it?

Josh should leave well alone. Yet for as long as he'd known Gabby, he'd felt keenly her sense of displacement and inadequacy. Her parents opposed her choices; she hadn't got along with her brother; she'd downplayed her closeness to Xander; she hadn't considered herself to be in the same league as the other law undergraduates yet had been reluctant to leave their halls of residence after she'd switched to the psychology programme. To Josh's mind, there was a strong element of self-sabotage involved, and it all came back to this house. Therefore, it didn't matter whether, in the long run, they sold it; what was important was that they acknowledged they had belonged here once.

An hour was all it took for Josh to establish that he'd been wrong and they might not have belonged there at all.

He was right on most other counts, though. The original Merton Hall had indeed been a stone castle, built towards the end of the fifteenth century and then slighted in 1643, during the First English Civil War. It was later rebuilt around the ruins in 1661, after 'The War of the Three Kingdoms' ended, and again in 1863 after a lightning strike caused a fire that destroyed sixty percent of the building. The contemporary Merton Hall was a hotchpotch of Tudor castle, Restoration and Victorian architecture—in Josh's opinion, a very handsome combination.

There were no records at all relating to the hall's history prior to 1643, but a little online research—sacrilege and modern heresy, hence conducted reluctantly—picked up the breadcrumb trail of shifting loyalties between local nobles, which, in 1600, had culminated in a siege on Merton Castle by the then landless Henry *Bouwes*, whose soldiers obliterated the castle's defences. Having gained access, Bouwes murdered Lord Pembroke—the rightful owner—and claimed the hand of Pembroke's daughter Elizabeth in marriage.

So it seemed Gabby's ancestors had acquired the hall by force, and to say Josh's research had not gone as well as he'd hoped was something of an understatement. But he wasn't ready to give up yet. According to the scholars of his discipline—and their sorely lacking excellent work in this library, which, ironically, spoke volumes; yes, Josh was taking it personally—sense of belonging had very little to do with ownership or duty. Rather, it was about acceptance, recognition and feeling valued, and Gabby and Andrew were working themselves into the ground in an effort to attain those from their father. But it was all superficial and impersonal, and while Josh couldn't reasonably expect an overt display of emotional attachment from Andrew, he should have felt a flicker of something from Gabby when they were up in the art studio.

It was then that it dawned on him: what was missing, or the most obvious manifestation of what was missing. Returning all of the books to their respective shelves, Josh dropped his gloves on the desk, à la throwing down the gauntlet, and picked up the phone, lifting the receiver to his ear. The smell of silver polish on his fingers made his nose crinkle.

"Finished so soon?"

"Almost, Cosgrove, almost. I wondered…are you terribly busy?"

***

Down to the bottom of the stairs and double back on yourself. It had sounded such an easy set of directions to follow, but the first two times George tried, he ended up outside the lift. It took retracing his steps almost all the way back to the art studio before he figured out Gabby had been talking about a different staircase. So that was four so far, and he'd only seen about a quarter of the house.

It was funny how knowing he was entering a library had him walking on tiptoes—his over-used calf muscles didn't thank him for it—and holding his breath. The light was different from the art studio, both dimmer and warmer, and the room was warm too. Very warm. George quietly closed the door, and stopped.

He'd expected to find Josh bent over an enormous antique oak desk, poring over a multitude of open books. Well, he got the desk right. As for Josh—George didn't think he'd ever seen him more relaxed, sitting in an armchair next to a crackling fire, feet resting on a stool, book in his hand—a peaceful yet alluring vision of his brainiac husband in his natural habitat.

"Aren't you melting?" George asked, by way of announcing his presence, and drew up alongside Josh's chair. "All you need now is a cravat and a smoking jacket."

Josh grinned up at him. "Hey, you."

"Hey, yourself." Between them they stretched up and bent down enough for their lips to briefly make contact before George went to sit in the chair on the other side of the fireplace. "This is a cosy setup."

"Yes." Josh closed the book and set it aside. "It's making me sleepy. How was your workshop?"

"Pretty good but a bit…I don't know. Lacklustre? And Clara and Matt turned up, though they didn't stay long, thank God. I only got about halfway done." Josh wouldn't ask what he was painting, knowing George was nervous about sharing before it was finished. The better a piece was going, the more he worried he might jinx it, and he would never destroy a painting or even paint over it. But this wasn't like his usual stuff, almost as if he'd commissioned himself, and he felt OK sharing. "I'm painting the forest."

"I thought you might. For Gabby?"

"Yeah. She kept finding excuses to leave us on our own. I think she was worried she was more of a hindrance than a help." George weighed it up. "To be honest, she was a bit distracting. I'm not sure why. I'm used to painting with her sitting next to me, but it was like my first art therapy session all over again. Really weird." George was having trouble pinpointing why he'd felt uneasy.

"Was it like being back at school?" Josh asked.

"I guess." George frowned. It made sense—it was a long time since he'd been an art student—but he couldn't help thinking there was more to it. "So, anyway, everyone else painted the local landscape—the view from the art studio is amazing. You can see for miles—the village, the forest, hills—and the light's perf…" He trailed off because Josh was nodding along, and he was listening, but… "You mean you actually looked out the window?"

"Yes, I did!" Josh said proudly. "We watched your snowball fight."

"You should've come and joined us."

"Not a chance." Josh didn't do snow…under normal circumstances.

"We had loads of fun." George couldn't help smiling as he thought back to how competitive Harriet had been, and also really good at using him as a human shield. He was sure around fifty percent of his aches and pains were down to bruises from their snowball fight, and he'd do it all again in a heartbeat. "So what have you been up to, apart from reading…whatever that is?" He couldn't make out the title for the cover's busy illustration.

"A poem by William Blake." Josh picked up the book and opened it, turning it to show George. "First edition—he illustrated it himself. He really was very talented."

"I'm sure he was," George said, along with an unspoken 'but you didn't come to the library just to read poetry', which Josh picked up on as if George had said it aloud.

"That's not *all* I've been up to. I've skimmed through the books about Merton Hall, and I've researched the earldom. *And* I've discovered Lord Bowes—not Gabby's dad, who's the fourteenth earl, and this was the third earl—took Merton Hall by force."

"That's um…"

"Surprising?"

"Yeah. Gabby's ancestors were a feisty bunch, huh?"

"Feistier than the living members of the Bowes family, that's for sure."

"Does that mean they're not the legal owners?"

"They probably are. The siege took place in 1600, and I imagine there are deeds somewhere that formalised the change of ownership, but it got me thinking. The third earl put up an almighty fight and lost his life trying to protect the castle, as it was then. Can you imagine if it was under siege now?"

"They'd just hand over the keys."

"My thoughts exactly. On which note, I've sent Cosgrove out to buy Christmas decorations."

"You— What?" George often had trouble following Josh's seemingly random changes in subject. They made sense to Josh, and eventually, with assistance, George could see how he'd got from A to B, but this one was head-the-ball crazy. "You sent Cosgrove for—"

"Christmas decorations, yes," Josh confirmed, like it was an everyday thing. "It occurred to me—I haven't checked the entire building, admittedly, but—I haven't seen so much as a solitary bauble."

"There's the tree out front," George argued. "And the lights on the willows along the drive."

"But they're *outside*, George. They're for show. Even the garlands around the windows are attached to the exterior sills. And I bet, if we visited the Bowes' living quarters, there'd be none there either."

George was still picturing the various rooms and corridors he'd been in for proof to the contrary, but Josh was right. "That's insane, this close to Christmas. Unless they're not religious? I mean, I know we're not religious and we still have decorations, but…"

"Who opens their house to the public in December and doesn't put up decorations? Even an understated tree in the entrance hall would have sufficed."

"Yeah, it'd need to be a big one." A normal-sized tree like the one they had at home would be lost in such an enormous space. An image of the row of overgrown conifers on the edge of the forest popped into George's head, all waving their spiny arms and shouting 'me, me, pick me' as Cosgrove advanced on them, knee-deep in snow, brandishing a glinting axe, tailcoat and vest and all.

George swallowed down a chuckle, blinking the vision away to focus on Josh again, who was watching him inquisitively, but it would take too much setting up to explain and then it wouldn't be funny anymore. He deflected. "I still can't believe I didn't notice. Although it took you twenty-four hours, so…" Josh stuck out his tongue, and George grinned back, but he was still struggling to see how a few fairy lights and a bit of tinsel were going to help.

"Shall I explain?" Josh suggested.

"Yeah. I think you better had."

"It's a symptom of their lack of emotional attachment—not just to the house, but to everything it symbolises. They went away to boarding school, and when they came home, they were with Martha. And I don't buy what Gabby said about their parents staying elsewhere while the place is overrun with tourists. They wouldn't have been here regardless—I remember Gabby telling me at uni that their parents always went away for Christmas.

I surmise that she and Andrew have never spent Christmas with them. They're lost children, seeking their parents' attention and approval."

"You're Freuding me."

Josh shrugged unapologetically. "It's what I do."

"Yep. And for once, I'd say you're right."

"Just the once?"

"Don't fish, Joshua. I'm agreeing with you. It fits with what Gabby was talking about earlier. Before the fox-hunting ban, they used to host hunters' balls and social nights and all kinds of stuff, but she was so matter-of-fact about it. Same with losing the house—if we were gonna lose ours…" George quickly pushed the thought away. He'd been through it once, a long, long time ago, and he never, ever wanted to go through it again.

"We'd fight tooth and claw," Josh finished for him. "It won't happen, George."

"You can't be sure."

"I can, because I won't let it. Come on." Josh pushed the foot stool aside and got up, holding out his hand. "Let's go and get ready for dinner."

George raised an eyebrow. "It's only five o'clock."

"Ten past," Josh amended. "And it'll take us another ten to get to our room."

Dinner wasn't until seven. Even so, George took Josh's hand and let himself be pulled out of the chair, straight into a hug. "I'm OK," he said. His brain glitched when he thought about losing what it had taken him so long to find—a secure home and a family with Josh, his best friend…his everything—but he really did feel OK. "I love you."

"Good." Josh pressed a kiss to George's temple. "I love you too. Shall we?"

Chapter Twelve

THEIR ROOM WAS an ice box after the cosy warmth of the library. The curtains billowed like the dark sails of an olde-worlde pirate ship and were next to useless against the draught from the gust forcing its way through the gaps around the ill-fitting windows. Josh had heard the library chimney howling, but he wasn't prepared for quite how extreme the weather had become in those few short hours.

"I hope Cosgrove made it back safely," he mused aloud. He shut the curtains again, pulling one over the other. It made not a jot of difference. His hair was still blowing all over the place.

"Did you say something?" George called from the bathroom. He appeared in the doorway, face half-covered in foam and a razor in his hand.

"Cosgrove," Josh said. "Do you think he's back yet?"

"Ah. Because of the wind." George disappeared back into the bathroom. "You could always call and ask."

He didn't want to be a pest, but George had suggested it, so it was probably a reasonable course of action. Josh picked up the phone, pressing the hash key as he put the receiver to his ear: no dial tone, no ringing. "Maybe the storm's taken the phones out," he speculated, knowing how ridiculous it was as he said it. Even if the overhead lines had been blown down, it was an internal system, and the lights were working, so the house still had power.

He stared at the bell by the door, pondering his options. Somehow, ringing it felt like taking advantage—more so than if he used the phone. However, he did now have two reasons to call Cosgrove or whoever was standing in as butler in his absence. Or perhaps Cosgrove had sent someone else for the decorations.

That was more likely. After all, wasn't the butler the most senior member of the household staff?

Deciding against the bell, Josh unhooked his jacket from the back of the door, and called, "I'm going to see what I can find out," already on his way, just in case George questioned if he really needed to or suggested he wait. He didn't need to, and his guilt for his underhanded manoeuvre steadily grew as he descended the stairs, to the extent he'd have turned around and gone straight back up to wait for George, were it not for the mayhem that slowed his steps almost to a complete stop. The house staff hurried back and forth, casting worried glances at one another as they passed. A few of the guests were huddled around the tables towards the front of the hall, while the sofas had just the one occupant, completely oblivious to all the comings and goings.

"Gabby?" Josh had said it quite loudly, but she didn't seem to have heard him. Taking care not to startle her, he walked over to where she was perched on the end of a sofa—the same one on which he'd spent the morning—face downturned, hands clasped around a scrunched-up white handkerchief. He stopped in front of her but kept his distance. "Gabby? What's the matter?"

Sniffling, she glanced up briefly, not quite meeting his gaze, and then looked away. "The studio…" Just saying that much stole what little control she had. She chewed her lip and tried again. "I went up to check everything was tidy for tomorrow, and she…" The lip-chewing didn't save her this time. She pressed the handkerchief to her nose and mouth and gulped down air.

"Mr. Sandison-Morley."

Resting his hand on Gabby's arm, Josh turned to acknowledge Cosgrove, spotting the enormous crate of Christmas decorations against the far wall.

"I tried calling you a few moments ago, but it would seem a fuse has blown and put our phone system out of operation."

That answered both of Josh's prior questions.

"I'd have come up, but there were, err…more pressing matters." Cosgrove eyed Gabby, who didn't seem to have noticed he was there either, and then beckoned to Josh.

"I'll be back in a moment," Josh said, waiting for Gabby's nod indicating she'd heard him. When it was apparent none was forthcoming, he followed Cosgrove away from the sofas and past the tables, closer to the decorations. There was quite a haul.

"How much did Her Ladyship tell you?" Cosgrove asked quietly.

"Not a lot. What's going on?"

"I'm not entirely sure at this stage. Her Ladyship discovered one of the guests in the studio. A window had been left open, and sleet had come in. Her Ladyship thinks the woman slipped and hit her head."

"So…she's unconscious?" Josh asked. Cosgrove didn't respond, but his head moved slightly from side to side. "She's dead?"

"Yes. I'm sorry to say she is."

"Hmm. Interesting." Josh looked back at Gabby, still with the handkerchief clutched in her hands. It was an impressive performance.

"I'm afraid we've had to cancel the evening's entertainment," Cosgrove said.

"Oh, of course." Josh didn't believe a word of it.

"We're also postponing dinner by an hour. That should give the police sufficient time to assure themselves nothing untoward happened."

"How convenient," Josh muttered.

"I beg your pardon?"

"Erm…I mean, they got here fast."

"Ah, yes," Cosgrove confirmed. "They were very prompt."

Josh nodded, still not buying it, and casually looked around the hall. "They're up there now, are they?"

"Yes. Now, if you will excuse me…"

Josh smiled amenably at the butler, who dipped his head in a half-bow, turned, and marched off towards the west wing. Josh watched until he was out of sight before returning to Gabby and endeavouring to get into the spirit of the evening. He hadn't expected her to play a role in it, but after his earlier observations, it was encouraging. Perhaps she wasn't as apathetic as he'd initially thought.

"How are you doing? Can I get you anything?"

"No, but thank you," she answered thickly.

"Where's Howie?"

"He's taken the children home. I don't want them here with... all of this going on. It won't do them any good." She looked up at him, eyes bloodshot and swollen, lip quivering—a *very* convincing performance. "I can't believe this is happening, and on our first weekend. I suppose I should've realised... It's no damn wonder everything we do is doomed to failure."

"You keep saying that, but I don't understand why."

"Father—he should never have opened that blasted room."

"You can't honestly believe it's cursed."

"Then it's what? Coincidence?"

"Or a self-fulfilling prophecy, perhaps?" Josh said it as if he were wildly speculating. Performance or not, he wasn't going to entertain nonsense of haunted rooms or cursed rooms or whatever other supernatural forces Gabby claimed were responsible.

"I should have invited Xander for the weekend. We could have got to the bottom of this once and for all, before..." She didn't finish, but Josh could've filled in the blank quite easily.

"Yes, you should invite Xander. At least he'd get a conversation—the entire place is devoid of life."

"It's that room, Josh."

"No, it's not, Gabby. It's you, and Andrew, and your parents. You loathe this house and begrudge your obligation to save it, yet you loathe the idea of parting with it just as much, so you're stuck in a repeating cycle of trying not very hard to do either."

Gabby wasn't crying anymore, which was positive. On the other hand, she was getting quite cross but calmly restated her position. "All of our problems started when that room was opened, and as soon as the police have finished with it, we're sealing it up again—for good."

"Well, you should do what you feel is necessary." Josh left her to interpret as she saw fit.

"We will. Now, if we're done here, I need to inform my parents." She stood but didn't go anywhere, waiting for him to move out of her way even though she could quite easily have stepped around him. He gestured for her to pass.

"Good job, by the way," he said.

She halted mid-step and turned back. "What?"

"This." Josh circled his hand to signify. Gabby frowned and shrugged. "The murder mystery. It's really clever."

She came back, scrutinising him until he began to feel like a naughty child attempting to lay the blame for his wrongdoing elsewhere. "You think this is all an act?" Her tone modulated—holding back annoyance or amusement? It was hard to tell, so he shrugged neutrally, not wishing to dispel the fiction but equally not ready to fully immerse himself in the role of amateur sleuth. "Josh, a woman is dead!"

"Right, yes. She slipped and banged her head…or did someone hit her with a blunt object? No, scratch that. We have to figure it out for ourselves, don't we?"

Gabby laughed in disbelief. "I really thought you'd have learned to empathise or at the very least a bit of tact by now. Even Xander's accomplished that much."

He nodded slowly, crinkling his eyes in what he hoped looked like empathy and refusing to react to her remark. She'd taken it too far, but she probably wasn't any more comfortable with play-acting than he was. "So where are they? The police? Paramedics? Undertakers?"

"I'm not having this discussion," Gabby snapped and stormed off in much the same fashion Harriet had the previous evening when Howie told her they weren't walking the dogs. At the corner, she paused and looked back at him. "Not that you deserve an explanation, but she'd lost a lot of blood, and I didn't know if it was an accident or something more sinister. I called the police—if you don't believe me, go and look." With one last glower, she departed for real, her heels clacking at speed along the corridor.

The other guests, who had paused to watch and listen, returned to their mumbled conversations.

Another servant scurried past.

Josh chewed his cheek and considered his next move. There was little point in pursuing Gabby. She'd presented her piece of the puzzle. *Who to question next?* Short answer: no-one, not until he'd collected George and brought him up to speed. He should do that now—go back up to their room, finish getting ready for dinner and nurse his bruised ego so it didn't flare up later when he was in the company of less-understanding others. *No empathy? How bloody rude!*

However, while his body pointed him at the stairs, his brain had an entirely different agenda.

Just a quick peek at the 'scene of the crime', get a head start.

It wasn't competing; it was entering into the spirit of the event. Or that was what he told himself as he detoured via the west wing. He'd found plans for all three versions of Merton Hall in one of the books and had memorised the map of its contemporary form, thus had no trouble finding his way back to the library, or, rather, the spiral staircase just before it, but that was as far as he was getting.

"Can I help you, sir?" A burly male in realistic police uniform, complete with night stick and jabbering radio, stepped towards him, arms spread just enough to imply trying to sneak past wasn't advisable.

"Erm…" Josh leaned to the side, peering around the man. "I think I left my pen in the library earlier."

The 'police officer' glanced behind him at the library door. After a moment's consideration, he nodded—"Quick as you can"—and allowed Josh to pass.

"Thank you," he said and darted inside, pushing the door to but not closing it, so he could listen whilst he pretended to search, silently circling the desk and poking down the side of the chair cushion in the event anyone was watching. The fire had dwindled to ashy embers, lending a suitably sinister ambience to his enactment, completed when he slid the pen from his pocket, where it had been the entire time, but it was all in vain. No-one was watching, and he couldn't hear a thing.

"Found it," he said as he exited the room, holding the pen up for inspection. The so-called police officer nodded. "Erm…may I ask what's going on?"

"Nothing you need concern yourself with." There was movement on the stairs he was guarding, and he ushered Josh past. "Be on your way, sir."

Josh obeyed, or gave the illusion of obeying. As soon as he rounded the corner, he stopped and leaned against the wall, listening, on this occasion thankful for the building's excellent acoustics, which allowed him to hear almost every word of the murmured conversation.

"They're bringing her down in the service lift," said a new voice—a woman's, possibly. "Can you get some tape up?"

"Yes, Ma'am. Where do you want it?"

"Across here will do. Ben's taken care of the upper levels already. Then you might as well clock off."

"If you're sure, Ma'am…"

"Yeah. The SOCO's finishing up now so everything's secure overnight. CID aren't coming until the morning. Go on. I'll see you in about an hour. You can get the first round in."

"Will do, Ma'am." Footsteps headed in Josh's direction. "What are you drinking?" the man asked, but Josh didn't get to find out. He speed-walked back the way he'd come, making it to the staircase up to their room as the service lift descended into view behind the concertina doors.

By now panting and around fifteen percent convinced this was the real deal, Josh watched over the banister. He was dizzy from too much caffeine and not enough oxygen, but he was going nowhere until he'd seen what was in that lift. The doors opened, and two people in grey uniforms silently wheeled out a stretcher carrying a lumpy body bag. One stopped to shut the lift doors, and then they were gone.

Josh gave himself a few seconds to catch his breath, and review all he'd seen and heard, before he set off along the picture-filled corridor, back to their room, to tell George.

Chapter Thirteen

GEORGE LISTENED WITHOUT comment and continued to dress while Josh told him about his argument with Gabby and what was going on. As he talked, Josh became increasingly animated—wide hand gestures, pacing back and forth, fiddling with his hair—all sure signs his thought processes were ramping up. When he finally stopped—by which point George was fully dressed and ready to go—he went to use the bathroom.

"You think it's a real murder, don't you?" George called through the door. The toilet flushed, and Josh emerged, rubbing his hands dry on a towel. "You think someone's actually died."

"Or it's a brilliantly elaborate hoax." Josh deposited the towel and shut the door. "Did you speak to any of the other artists earlier?"

"A few of them. I wonder who it is." George visualised the semicircle of easels; only three of the twenty had been occupied by men, so knowing the victim—or alleged victim—was a woman didn't narrow the field much.

"We should go downstairs, see who's there," Josh suggested. He was at the door before George could even draw breath to answer.

"I don't know if that's a good idea. Maybe they want us to stay up here."

"And spend the next two hours confined to our rooms? No. Cosgrove will have arranged somewhere for us all to go, and if he hasn't, we'll just sit in the entrance hall." Josh turned the doorknob, then paused, looking back past George and frowning. "Coffee. That's something else she needs to do." He opened the door and stepped outside.

"Huh?" George followed him out, locking up behind him.

"Coffee and tea in the rooms," Josh explained. "It wouldn't occur to Gabby and Andrew to provide it because they're used to twenty-four-hour room service."

"That's part of the package for these weekends, though," George pointed out.

"Yes, but it's novel to us commoners."

"I bet some of them have got Cosgrove and his staff running up and down the stairs at all hours."

"Oh, I quite agree. There will always be some who abuse it, but most will feel like we do and use it as little as possible, not wanting to add to the servants' workload."

"Says he who sent the butler out in gale-force winds to buy Christmas decorations…"

Josh smiled demurely and said no more.

They reached the bottom of the stairs and stopped to assess the situation. A couple of guests were sitting on one of the sofas, another couple at one of the tables.

"Speaking of decorations…" George pointed to the stash near the front doors.

"Hmm, yes. I saw those before. Short of putting them up ourselves, I can't see them making it out of that crate now. The best laid plans…"

"Schemes," George corrected. Josh eyed him curiously, so he went on, "O' mice an' men gang aft agley, an' lea'e us nought but grief an' pain, for promis'd joy!"

Josh's mouth fell open. "We need to talk."

"Ha! You think you have the monopoly on classic poetry?"

"Erm…I think…" Josh shook his head. "I don't know what I think."

George laughed and took his hand. "I love it when you're lost for words." They walked down towards the wider section of the hall. "Makes me feel less inadequate."

"You're not inadequate, George."

"You know what I mean."

"I do." Josh hummed in thought. "Robert Burns, yes?"

"Yeah."

"I haven't read much of his work."

"I haven't read *any* of it, but you don't get to study in Aberdeen for three years without attending a Burns night…or three."

"Ah. Did you eat haggis?"

"I did. Fair fa' your honest, sonsie face, great chieftain o' the puddin' race."

Josh grinned widely. "That's delightful. Do you know any more?"

"Bits and pieces."

"Go on," Josh urged.

"Nope."

"Coward."

"Yep." No way was he making a fool of himself in front of an audience, or not sober.

"You know, I'm almost tempted to try haggis," Josh said as they walked over to the sofas.

"You won't like it," George told him with certainty. It would be 'a bit too spicy' or 'a curious texture' but also 'really nice, George'—code for 'God, this is awful'. But maybe he'd give it a try for Burns night—without the Scotch. Those Aberdeen hangovers had put him off hard liquor for life.

They chose the sofa opposite the only other one in use and exchanged greetings with their fellow guests. George vaguely knew the woman from the art workshop—they'd chatted briefly while they were cleaning their brushes—although not the guy sitting with her, who was absorbed by something on his phone but glanced up to acknowledge them.

"Have you heard?" asked the woman—Amber.

"Yeah. Do you know who it is?"

Amber nodded and her eyes lit up. "That journalist."

"Clara?"

Josh laughed and clapped his hands. "Perfect! Couldn't happen to a nicer…" George gave him a warning glare, which shut him up for the time being.

"What happened? Do you know?"

Amber shook her head. "No, but look at this." She reached over and took the phone out of the guy's hand. "Sorry, this is my husband, Mark."

"Hi, Mark. I'm George, and this is Josh…my husband." He hated that he still hesitated in telling people that.

Josh and Mark exchanged quiet hellos whilst Amber did something with the phone and then handed it to George. He scanned the first couple of lines.

"Guess it's not a hoax, then."

"What's that?" Josh asked. George held the phone between them so they could both see. "What the hell?" Josh took it from him and scrolled down, and down.

So it was true. Clara Coltrane was dead, and the news was all over Twitter, with some leaving 'RIP' messages while others were saying 'good riddance' or worse—a couple of the tweets were really mean, to the point where even Josh muttered, "Disgusting." For as much as she'd pissed them off at breakfast, she deserved some respect. Her family and friends would see those tweets.

"That was quick." Josh handed Amber's phone back and dug his own out of his pocket. "Too quick." He unlocked the browser and—predictably—went straight to the BBC website, local news page. George leaned in and read it too.

DEAD WOMAN AT MERTON HALL THOUGHT TO BE CLARA COLTRANE

A woman, believed to be controversial journalist Clara Coltrane, has died at Merton Hall during an open weekend.

Earlier this evening, police were called to the large stately home in the Peak District by Lady Gabrielle

Porter, daughter of the current earl, Lord Charles, and Lady Catherine Bowes, following the discovery of the deceased woman in the hall's west tower.

A police spokesperson could not confirm the identity of the dead woman but said: "We are treating the death as suspicious."

Josh closed down the browser and locked his phone, looking across to the other sofa. "I didn't catch your name."

"Oh, sorry! It's Amber."

"Good to meet you," he said quite curtly but must have realised he'd been rude because he pulled himself together and affected his 'interested' smile. "Enjoying yourself?"

Amber nodded. "It's been good so far, except...you know..."

"Hmm." Josh did the sensible thing and shut up. He sucked at small talk in general, but he was in the same boat as all the non-artists, who hadn't had a chance to properly socialise yet; that might change, if they ever made it to dinner.

For a while, the four of them sat in silence, and then George and Amber both asked at the same time, "Has anyone seen the photographer?"

No-one had, and the silence resumed. More guests arrived, gradually filling the sofas and tables, their murmured conversations like the buzz of a beehive. George glanced sideways at Josh, ready to nudge him if he was too obviously people-watching, but he wasn't watching them at all. George followed the direction of his gaze.

Gabby and Andrew stood, heads close together, shielding their mouths with their hands as they talked. Understandably, they were both very upset; this had to be awful for them: left in charge for the first time and now a woman was dead—a journalist no less. There was no way they could've kept that out of the media. Andrew was so tense he looked like he'd fire off like a rubber band at any second, while Gabby's face was blotchy from crying.

Their conversation went on for several minutes, during which the hall filled with guests, who remained on their feet as there was nowhere left to sit. Like Josh and George, their curiosity must have got the better of them because it was still more than an hour until their rescheduled dinner. Eventually, Andrew beckoned to one of the servants and they left together; Gabby came over to address the gathering.

"Should I go and check on Andrew, do you think?" Mark asked Amber. "He looks stressed to hell."

She shook her head. "Let's hear what Gabby's got to say first."

"You know them?" George asked.

"Mark went to school with Andrew," Amber explained quickly; Gabby was waiting to speak.

"Good evening, everyone. If you haven't heard already, I'm afraid there's very sad news. Clara Coltrane, a journalist from *Country Life* magazine who kindly agreed to write a feature on us, died earlier this evening. We're not sure of the circumstances at this time. Matt—her photographer—is presently helping the police with their inquiries, after which they may need to talk to some of you.

"Therefore, regrettably, we will not be holding our murder mystery event. I understand this is quite a disappointment for many of you, and we will gladly refund you, should you wish to leave us before the end of the weekend. We very much hope you will continue your stay.

"To confirm, this evening's new arrangements are: dinner at eight in the great hall, after which you'll have full access to the house apart from my family's private quarters and the west wing, which the police have cordoned off whilst they complete their investigation. Please do ask the staff should you need any refreshments. Thank you."

Gabby sped away, patently averting her eyes as she passed Josh and George.

"That's my fault," Josh said. George had figured as much, although he hadn't expected Josh to freely admit it. "I need to apologise. Excuse me." He got up and went after her.

"What did he do?" Amber asked.

"It's…complicated." George wasn't fobbing her off, or that wasn't his intent. If he tried to explain how Josh had upset Gabby, he'd have to start with them being at uni together, and Xander's role, and why, actually, Gabby owed Josh an apology for taking a Xander-related jab at him, and…well, it *was* complicated, but Amber looked like she felt fobbed off, so George just said, "Josh can be quite abrupt," which she'd already heard for herself.

"Gotcha." Amber and Mark shared a knowing glance that turned into giggles, both covering their mouths when they realised it was a bit inappropriate. "Mark's exactly the same," Amber said. "Aren't you?" He nodded regretfully. "But you have to be in your job."

"What do you do?" George asked.

"District Crown Prosecutor."

"A lawyer?"

"Barrister."

George decided against asking if he'd known their friend Jess. Mark had probably still been in uni when Jess was working for the Crown Prosecution Service—the guy only looked about thirty—and it was a large organisation. "I'm guessing you're pretty ambitious?"

"I wouldn't say I'm overly ambitious." He sought confirmation from Amber, and she nodded. "I used to work for the Crown Court advocacy service, which I loved, but this job came up, so I applied for it, and I got it. Now I'm in charge of the prosecutors in my local magistrates service."

"Sounds tough."

"It is sometimes. Some of my team are my buddies from before I took this job, and they're great, you know? They work really hard, but I feel weird ordering them around."

"I can imagine." That was how George had felt on the ranch. All the guys knew more than he did, and he preferred to work alongside them, but from time to time, he had to be the boss and do the hard boss things, like firing people. That was the worst. Thankfully, he'd only had to do it twice.

"How about you, George? What line of work are you in?"

"I'm a labourer on an educational farm—mucking out, teaching kids about animal welfare…" People didn't usually have a clue what his job entailed, which was why he always explained when they asked, and they were often judgemental about his choice of career, but someone had to do it. "It's a lot of fun," he vindicated.

"Hard work, though," Amber said. "I worked on a farm the summer after I left school. Picking lettuce."

"Wow. That really is hard work."

"It is, but it's a walk in the park compared to bringing up kids. We've come away this weekend to get a break from them before Christmas or I'll be sneaking them into Santa's sack so he can take them back to the North Pole with him."

George chuckled. "Are they young?"

"The eldest is five, then the next one's two, and the baby's three months. Have you got any?"

"Yeah. A daughter. She's nearly seventeen, though. This is the first time we've left her home alone."

"Aww. I bet you're worried."

"A bit. Trying not to ring her every five minutes…" That was a slight exaggeration—he'd only called Libby four times, relenting when she put Sean on the phone and demanded he confirm everything was OK. "I'll be glad to get back home," George said. "I don't like being away from her."

Amber smiled in sympathy. "Whereas I can't wait to go back to work for a break. I'm a buyer for a ceramics company. That's how I got into art, and I make my own stuff—carved designs, mugs and trinket pots and things like that. I sell online, but it's just a hobby. I'd love to do it full-time." Amber laced her fingers with Mark's. "That's why you went for promotion, isn't it, babe?" Mark nodded and smiled; no regret there. They obviously loved each other very much, or else why would a lawyer choose to come on a murder mystery weekend? It had to be a bit of a busman's holiday for the guy.

"How about Josh?" Amber asked. "What does he do?"

"He's a psychologist."

"Oh!"

George waited for the customary wild speculation about Josh's mind-reading capabilities, accompanied by whomever they were talking to asking if Josh could guess what they were thinking, except he wasn't there to entertain or enlighten—or infuriate, as was more often the outcome—so it killed the conversation stone dead. "I'm gonna see if I can get a beer in this place. Would you guys like one?"

"Yeah, that'd be great, actually. Do you want a hand?" Mark offered.

"No, you stay there. I can manage. Amber?"

"Yes, beer for me too, please."

"Cool. I'll see what I can do. Won't be long."

Chapter Fourteen

GABBY, CAN I talk to you?" Josh caught up with her at the bottom of the east wing stairs. She stopped walking but kept her back to him, making him work for it. He didn't think he was entirely to blame for their argument, but one of them needed to make the first move towards fixing it. "I'm sorry for upsetting you. You're right—I was insensitive about…everything. Believe it or not, I was trying to help."

"When you know nothing of this house?"

"Actually, that's not strictly—" Josh had the sense to quit; his pedantry could only make it worse. "No, you're right. Before this weekend, I didn't even know where it was, but not because I don't care." Quite the opposite. He researched everything—compulsively, according to George—but he'd intentionally steered clear of researching Gabby's family, having perceived her parents' treatment of her as abusive. He knew better now; their family was dysfunctional and in need of some form of intervention, but her father wasn't abusive. His grief had festered and become irrational. But that was an argument for another day.

"And," he added, "I'm sorry for being so dismissive of what you've been through this evening. I thought it was part of the festivities." Awful as the circumstances were—he was taking it at face value until proven otherwise—he was pleased the murder mystery was off. He'd have gone along with it so as not to hurt Gabby and Andrew's feelings, but he had no interest in solving fictitious crimes, irrespective of whether those crimes were grounded in fact.

"All right." Gabby turned to face him and mustered a bit of a smile. "Apology accepted. I'm sorry too, for comparing you to

Xander. I don't really understand why you see it as an insult, but I knew that was how you'd take it—not that I'd planned to say it in advance."

"I know." He tentatively stepped towards her, and she to him, and they hugged, which became a little less awkward each time they did it. "Are you coping?"

"I'd like to say yes, but I fear I'll break down once everyone's gone to bed. I've not been sleeping well of late as it is."

"Any particular reason?"

"Howie's mother is ill, and they're a closer family than we are. I know that isn't saying much, but it's more that his mother is in charge over there, and that's the way it's always been. His father is something of a loose cannon—he's struggled with addiction all of his adult life—so he's given an allowance in return for which he has to attend public functions and keep his mouth shut."

"Like Prince Philip," Josh joked, and Gabby smiled for real.

"Look, are you in a rush to get back to George, or do we have time for a coffee? It seems silly us standing out here and chatting."

"Coffee sounds great."

Gabby unlocked the door and pointed him towards a sitting room. "Go and sit. I'll bring it in when it's done."

Josh did so, slowly, taking in the Bowes' living quarters, which were not what he'd expected. The furnishings were still upmarket, all bespoke items, but they'd been chosen for comfort over aesthetics, creating a jumble of colours that didn't coordinate. For all of that, once Josh sat on the sofa, he decided he was staying put for the evening. If someone brought him a blanket, he'd have gladly slept there.

"Has the couch swallowed you?" Gabby asked on her return a few minutes later.

"Alas, it's the story of my working life," Josh lamented.

Gabby peered down at him. "I can barely see you for all the cushions." She handed him his coffee. "Cappuccino."

"Thanks." He sipped it right away. "Mmm, that's good." He sighed and sank another couple of inches, hearing Gabby's giggle from beyond the cushion barricade. "This is so comfortable. Where's it from?"

"Some little shop in London."

"Expensive?"

"Not astronomical. They make the sofa to the exact size you specify and send you a colour swatch. Of course, if you were thinking of buying a sofa from there, you wouldn't need the swatch—Mum decided she'd have one cushion in each of the eighteen colours available."

"Eighteen?" Josh repeated. That would explain the test-card effect playing havoc with his vision. However, as he'd suspected, the sitting room was devoid of Christmas decorations. "When are your parents back from France?"

"Not until January. Why do you ask?"

Josh sipped his coffee, wondering how much he dared say when they'd made up not five minutes ago. It would be better to get it over with, assuming he could deploy some of the tact he allegedly didn't have.

"I realised something this afternoon. I don't know if you're aware of it too, and I have a theory. May I share?"

Gabby shrugged her consent.

"How many Christmases have you spent with your parents?"

"Three. We went with them to France a couple of times in our teens, and we spent Christmas here one year. Well, Andrew and I were here every Christmas. They weren't."

"What was different about that year?"

Gabby inhaled deeply. Whatever she was about to tell him had flipped a switch, and she knew what he was getting at. She closed her eyes as she exhaled. "There was heavy snow and all the flights were cancelled."

"But it was normal for you, wasn't it? You didn't feel like you were missing out."

"No. We weren't short of gifts, and they were well considered. I think they realised Nanny and the staff could provide a better Christmas for us. It doesn't mean we aren't hurt by them choosing a couple of weeks of skiing over spending time with us. When I was away at school and then university, I didn't see my parents, literally, from one year to the next. I actually see more of them now, when I live a hundred miles away and work fifty hours a week, than I ever did, and they dote on Harriet and Xander..."

"But not enough to want to be here with them at Christmastime," Josh finished.

Gabby shook her head. "As you say, it's normal for us, and the children don't think anything of it. As long as the four of us are together for Christmas, that's what counts. And Nanny's spending this Christmas with us too." Gabby smiled, though she was tearful. "I miss her."

"Yes, that was something of a flying visit earlier," Josh remarked, still probing and hating himself a little for doing so.

"She stayed for all of lunch—of course, you wouldn't know about that..." She mimicked his blithely sarcastic tone. "Don't worry, Nanny hasn't abandoned us. She spent the afternoon with her friends in the village, though she says they're all old ladies these days."

"Out of interest, how old is she?"

"Ageless, like Nurse Matilda." The unspent tears made Gabby's eyes twinkle. "That's what she used to tell us, anyway. I'd say probably her early seventies. The children asked the same thing—do you know, they had no idea who Nurse Matilda is."

"Appalling," Josh said, and they both laughed. "Your children seem very happy and well-balanced."

"Ignorance of classical children's stories and Harriet's tantrums notwithstanding?"

Josh smiled in empathy—yes, he had it—but stopped short of comparing their daughters' teenage strops, lest they descend into mindless tit-for-tat when the conversation was going better than he'd anticipated. "Do they help put up the Christmas decorations at home?"

"What you're really asking is, do we have Christmas decorations at home?"

Josh grimaced, although it had been a poorly disguised question.

"Yes, we do," Gabby confirmed. "I'll admit they're Howie's doing, not mine. He wants to install one of those huge light displays—you know, the ones that flash in time to music? He loves those. But, like here, Porter Lodge is a World Heritage site, so no gaudy light displays allowed."

"What killjoys!" Josh played up his outrage to keep Gabby smiling—a particularly beautiful sight after their glum, worrisome day. Time to own up, but he finished his coffee first and confessed to the cup. "Did you, erm, notice the box of decorations in the hall?"

"Yes. Something to do with you, I take it?"

Josh nodded. "I asked Cosgrove to make it so." He attempted to sit up a little straighter, hoping he could ease his way out of the sofa, soon realising he wasn't getting out of it unaided. "He's very good, isn't he? Cosgrove, I mean." Maybe if he shuffled forward… no. "Nothing is too much—oh, for goodness' sake." Josh gave up and joined in with Gabby's laughter at his expense.

"Here, give me that," she said, taking his cup away and setting it down before she grabbed his hands and heaved with all her tiny might. It took a few tries and a count of three so they were working together, but on the last attempt, Josh popped from the sofa like a cork from a Champagne bottle.

"Thanks." He stared down at the dip he'd been sitting in. "I think it might actually have digested me whole if I'd stayed there any longer, but what a way to go!" Gabby squeezed his arm. She was still giggling on and off. "All right, so now that's out of the way, how can I help you this evening? Other than being a perfect guest?"

"You should perhaps aim for something more achievable to start with?" Gabby teased.

Josh huffed, but he had no right to be offended when he'd fretted the morning away, missed most of her tour and then thanked her for giving him exclusive access to the estate library by sending her butler on a mission *and then* caused a stand-up row.

"If you're serious…" she said.

"I am."

"Even if it means breaking the law?"

"Erm…it depends what you mean by breaking the law."

"Well, not exactly breaking the law. Interfering with a crime scene."

"I'm not sure George will be happy with it."

"I'm not asking you to conceal evidence or anything like that. It's just that the police aren't coming back until tomorrow—they have their Christmas party this evening—and the art studio is off-limits. All the guests' paintings are still on their easels, and if I can't get them out—"

"There will be no art session in the morning."

Gabby nodded. "So…I'm going to leave it as long as I can, but if they haven't given us the all-clear by, say, nine-thirty tomorrow…"

"OK."

"I'm only asking you to help me, not go in there on your own."

"I said OK."

"It's too much for me to carry, and I don't want—"

"Gabby, I said OK."

"You— Oh. Thank you."

"You're welcome. But I'm curious—why me rather than Howie or Andrew—or George, for that matter?"

"Firstly, you won't freak out if anything unexplainable occurs."

"Just because we can't explain something, it doesn't mean—"

"Yes, I know!" Gabby interrupted sharply.

"Sorry." Josh bowed his head, feeling a little sheepish. It had to be their studying together that brought his argumentative streak to the fore. "Was there a secondly?"

"Yes. Secondly, you know how to handle yourself with the police."

Josh couldn't argue with that. He'd worked with the police often enough that they didn't intimidate him as much as they did other people, although they still had the power of the law on their side, and he and Gabby would, potentially, be breaking it. But there was more. "Thirdly?" Josh prompted.

Gabby cleared her throat, but not nervously. She was becoming emotional again. "I know we've had our differences, today in particular, but there is no-one I trust more to fight in my corner."

Josh blushed so hard he started to sweat. "I agreed already, didn't I? You don't need to butter me up."

Chapter Fifteen

"Well, it's no Hogwarts, that's for sure," George heard Mark mutter to Amber as the serving staff herded them into the great hall. It was a fair point; the hall could have comfortably seated around a hundred diners—another twenty if they had short arms—but it was nowhere near as big as the name implied. There was no top table either, and the dais was bare, which George probably wouldn't have noticed but for Josh pointing out the lack of Christmas decorations. A row of small, lit trees would have been the perfect touch.

Perhaps it was simply the absence of personal effects, but the longer they were there, the greater George's sense of being an imposter. While Josh had been with Gabby, George had chatted with a few of the other guests—mostly about Clara's death, with everyone having a different theory of what had happened to her. A lawyer, a doctor, a college lecturer, so many teachers…all those high-paid professionals, and there he was, George Morley, farm labourer from a council estate, trying to hold his own. He might have been joking about feeling inadequate earlier, but he felt so out of place it wasn't funny.

In Gabby's and Andrew's defence, they sat among the 'riff-raff'; Gabby in particular was watchful of their guests, sending servers to check on anyone whose glass needed replenishing. They'd also stocked up on beer, which, Cosgrove said, wasn't usually available in the house, and the food was excellent.

The starters were quite ordinary—a choice between mulligatawny soup, spinach and mushroom tart or some kind of liver mousse, which was actually just well whisked liver paté.

There were only two entrée options: roast game birds with sautéed vegetables and a not very vegetarian-sounding *steaks de seitan maison.* Roast game birds were, apparently, close enough to chicken in texture for Josh to not retch at the feel of the food in his mouth, so he was able to savour the taste. He even accepted an extra slice when it was offered and tolerated—with minimal face-pulling—the redcurrant and sloe gin jelly.

The vegan option turned out to be a deep-fried something, possibly bean curd, covered in herbs and spices, and it looked OK but received a mixed reception. One of the guests complained loudly that wet cardboard would've had more taste to it; Gabby overheard and was mortified. The next time one of the staff was nearby, Josh grabbed the salt mill from them and thrust it under the complainant's nose. Flustered, they ground the tiniest amount of salt over their food—not enough to make a difference—and thanked Josh for his concern.

"No problem at all," Josh said with a terrifying smile, which he toned down before he handed the salt back to the server, still managing to unnerve her. From there on, she gave Josh a wide berth, but he didn't notice, too busy watching and listening. A room full of people could keep him occupied for hours, so apart from that little hiccup, the meal remained incident free.

"I hate when they make you choose," George mumbled, tucking into his Eton Mess while enviously eyeing the cheese boards all around him. "This is really good, but—" A light tap on his shoulder startled him.

"I've saved a cheese board for your supper." Cosgrove was gone before George could thank him.

"How did he do that?" he asked Josh. "Is he one of yours?"

"One of my what?"

"Telepaths."

Josh slow-blinked. He didn't have to say it; they had the same conversation quite often. *It's not telepathy, it's basic psychology.*

"We've had an idea," Mark interrupted their moment. He and Amber were sitting opposite George and Josh and had been engaged in quiet conversation throughout the meal. Josh gestured for him to go on. "You say the police aren't coming back until the morning?"

"Correct."

"Well, maybe we could do a bit of digging around, see what we can find out."

"How do you propose we do that? There were no witnesses."

"Ah, but there are security cameras."

Josh automatically looked up and around the walls. "Where?"

"You're not a fan of art and sculptures, then?" Mark asked smugly.

Josh stopped searching the room and homed in on Mark. George braced.

"And you said this place had nothing on Hogwarts," Josh jibed lightly. George relaxed a little. "Show me."

Both men pushed their chairs away and walked to the end of the table, from where they set off together. George followed their stop-start progress around the perimeter of the room, as did a few other people. They examined at least a dozen paintings before they made it back to their seats.

"That's rather clever," Josh told George. "They're hidden in the beading on the frames."

"Did you think they'd be in the eyes?" George asked. He was kidding, but Josh's reaction confirmed he had thought that. George coughed into his hand.

"Are you laughing at me, Morley?"

"Nope."

"You are."

He wasn't, because he wanted to know where Mark and Amber had been going with their idea. "You were saying, Mark?"

"Yes, so we've got the security footage, plus—I don't know if you've been listening…" He subtly tilted his head at the other table, although it was impossible to figure out which person he was indicating. "She heard Clara on the phone at lunchtime. Quite a heated conversation, by all accounts."

"Whose accounts?" Josh asked.

"Just the one," Mark said. "Sorry. Turn of phrase."

"There must be others who overheard."

"You two could interview them," Amber suggested, pointing at Mark and Josh.

"Mark's a barrister," George explained before Josh questioned that too.

"Right, yes. That would work."

"Yeah." George frowned. Things seemed to have escalated very quickly from 'we've had an idea' to 'we should interrogate the guests'. "Why are you doing this again?" he asked.

"Because—" Josh began, but George cut him off.

"I wasn't asking you. I *know* why you're doing it. I want to know why they are."

Mark shrugged. "Helping out a friend."

"Mark and Andrew went to the same school," George said.

"Yes, I heard that part." Josh scrutinised the man. "So you're here out of a sense of duty, are you?"

"I wouldn't put it like that. I'm here for Amber, mostly, but Andrew promised an evening I'd enjoy, and you have to admit this is kind of fun."

"Ah, I see what's happening here," Josh said. "You're a manager."

"I'm not sure what it has to do with anything, but yes, I am."

"Promoted…hmm…about a year ago?"

"That's right."

"Which means you have a three-month-old child?"

Mark crossed his arms. "George told you."

"No." Josh turned away to intercept a server. "Hey, sorry to be a pest, but could I have another coffee, please?"

"Certainly, sir."

"Thank you." He turned back and examined Mark, who stared him dead in the eye, challenging him.

"Josh," George warned.

"It's all right," Mark said. "He's not going to tell us anything we don't know."

Josh shifted his gaze to Amber. "You didn't want him to go for promotion."

She almost nodded, but it turned into a head shake. "No. He did it so I could give up work to build my business."

"Business…arts and crafts of some sort?"

"Ceramics," Amber confirmed.

"See?" Mark said. "Everything you've said so far is word for word what we told George."

"Ah. You're waiting for me to pull a rabbit out of my hat. All in good time."

George rubbed his eyes, already weary of the posturing. This was what started the arguments and would have done so on this occasion, but Mark had a trick of his own.

"You're good," he said. "Very good."

"Thank you," Josh accepted graciously. "As are you. Your team's lucky to have you at the helm."

"Thank you," Mark said humbly, and then they were off, discussing their interview strategy and who they needed to talk to. Amber seemed quite happy listening, but once George recovered from his shock at the rapid de-escalation of conflict, he soon became bored and was pleased when the servers started clearing the tables so he had an excuse for a timeout. He used the bathroom and then went for a walk around the ground floor to stretch his legs, which were very stiff now, from sitting around for so long. He was much more physically active at home, and he'd eaten too much.

He completed a full circuit of the corridors and was on his way through the entrance hall when the doorbell rang. He kept going, but when it appeared no-one was coming to answer it, he backtracked and was almost at the door before Cosgrove came charging over.

"Thank you. I'll take it from here."

"Sure." George continued on his way, slowly, listening to the conversation, which was brief and not very informative, before he sped up again and returned to his companions in the great hall. "Guess who's just got back from the police station."

"Matt Shapiro?" Josh asked to check.

"Yep."

"How did he seem?"

"I didn't see him. I just heard Cosgrove talking to him and the police officer who brought him back."

"Had he been arrested?" Mark asked.

"I don't think so. The officer was treading lightly, telling him to take it easy."

"So he's been gone for three hours, but he wasn't in custody," Mark said, scratching his neck as he mulled it over. He refocused his gaze on Josh. "He knows something."

Josh nodded. "That does seem likely, and now we also know for sure Clara's death wasn't an accident."

"How?" George asked, trying to sound disinterested. He wished he'd kept quiet about Matt because Josh and Mark were talking in statements of fact, and George could hear warning bells. This was how it always began.

Mark answered. "They wouldn't have taken Matt away to question him unless he was initially a suspect. If they've released him…"

"There's a murderer on the loose," Josh finished.

Amber gasped. "What are we going to do?"

"Find out who it is," Josh said.

"Yeah," Mark agreed, flushing George's one last hope of common sense overriding obsession straight down the pan.

Mark, Josh and Amber chattered on enthusiastically, and George tuned them out until they became part of the drone of the many conversations happening around the room. But there was no escape; all he heard was Clara's name. Everyone was talking about her.

Josh turned to tell him something, took one look at him and also began listening, gaze drifting, eyebrows rising, eyes widening. "Witnesses," he said. George nodded to confirm he'd heard the same thing. "We need to find out what time Clara went up to the studio."

"Then we'll need access to the security footage," Mark said.

Josh was already on his feet. "I'll see what I can do. Cosgrove, do you have a moment?"

Chapter Sixteen

"I MUST APOLOGISE IN advance for the mess." Cosgrove unlocked the door and batted away a cobweb. He clicked the light switch, three times, to no effect.

"Presumably, you don't have any problems with trespassers," Josh remarked.

"We never have." Cosgrove pulled a small torch from his pocket and pointed it into the dark room, turning the newly disturbed dust into the resemblance of a swarm of fireflies. "His Lordship installed the CCTV because of hunt saboteurs. They were a peaceful, pleasant lot on the whole, but they were cunning—the only way we could stop them was by confronting them. They wouldn't get into a fight, you see, and we couldn't call the police without a disturbance of the peace."

Cosgrove continued talking as he opened the desk drawers, swiftly sifting, via torchlight, through the contents of each before moving on to the next. "His Lordship was ambivalent toward the hunt, and the rest of the family were outright against it—these are the ironies of tradition and privilege. It's imposed, whether one wants it or not. Here we are."

Cosgrove conjured a light bulb from somewhere and swapped out the blown one. Josh shut his eyes and waited for the burning sensation to pass before he opened them again.

"That's better."

"Yes, much." Now he could see why Cosgrove had apologised. The room was little more than a broom cupboard, fitted with an ancient computer connected to several square screens, all thick with dust. "Does that still work?"

"Let's see, shall we?" Cosgrove pushed the power button. It took a while, but eventually, the old hard drive noisily cranked to life.

"Sounds promising." Josh watched the monitor, raising an eyebrow when a white cursor's rapid flash appeared at the top of the screen. Behind him, Cosgrove was making quite a racket, tugging at the drawers of a stubborn metal filing cabinet.

"I need to fetch some oil," he said. "Will you be all right here?"

"Yes. You carry on."

He left, and Josh continued watching the screen: the MS DOS loading messages, followed by the 'press any key' prompt. He tapped the enter key, smiling nostalgically when the Windows 98 logo appeared.

"Hello, old friend. Long time no see." For an antique—in computer terms—the machine was surprisingly spritely, but it was still taking an age to start up, and the screen flicker was agony on the eyes. Josh looked away, giving the rest of the room a cursory inspection. There was a lot of admin-related stuff: sealed reams of paper, photocopier, antiquated—quite possibly dot-matrix—printer, a stack of old files...

"I wonder what's in those..." Listening out to make sure Cosgrove wasn't on his way back, Josh sidled over and picked up the top file, flicking it open.

The file contained several pages, all of the same blank table with columns labelled *Date*, *Time*, *Brief Description of Incident* and *Action Taken*. Josh set it to one side and picked up the next: the same photocopied table, but this time with scrawly writing by three different hands.

Almost every incident recorded had occurred on a Saturday, most consisting of 'X number of sabs gained access via... Left when asked' with 'N/A' in the *Action* column. A couple had required calls to the police, but on the whole, it was as Cosgrove had said: peaceful protesters who moved on when asked to by the estate's security.

The same was repeated in the next file, and the next, the dates going back some thirty years, with just one entry that deviated from the rest. It was a Christmas Eve, and Lord Etherington-Bowes had come to collect Xander, who'd refused to leave. His father, according to whomever recorded the incident, was drunk and caused injury to Cosgrove and Mrs. Perkins, with no indication how severe their injuries were. Police officers had escorted Xander's father and his chauffeur off the property.

"I see you got it working."

Josh leapt to his feet in surprise, leaving the file on top of the others and surreptitiously flipping it shut with his foot. "I… Yes." He'd been caught red-handed and braced for Cosgrove's verdict, but he didn't offer one, which was worse, because now Josh was waiting for the bomb to drop, and the tension was immense. He returned to the computer and scanned the coarsely pixelated desktop icons, one of which was a camera. He double-clicked it.

"That should do it," Cosgrove said and slid open the top drawer of the filing cabinet, then the one below, and so on through all four drawers. When he was done, he locked the cabinet again. "Will you be needing anything else?"

"Erm…" Josh stared, unseeing, at the screen. He shouldn't ask; it was irrelevant and none of his business. "Have you forgotten something?" He turned his head just enough that he could see Cosgrove's questioning frown. "The filing cabinet?"

"Oh!" The butler gave a small, disarming laugh. "No. I keep a list of all the jobs that need doing, and the filing cabinet has been on there for almost a decade. It's satisfying to finally be able to cross it off."

"I understand," Josh said, although he'd never have left something for that long. The software seemed to have loaded and successfully connected to the cameras. "How far back does the recording go, did you say?"

"Eight hours, I believe. I'm afraid I wouldn't know where to start."

"I'm not sure myself," Josh admitted. He knew his way around a computer, but he was no wiz. "Haven't the police requested access to this?"

"Not yet. They were in rather a rush to get to their celebration this evening."

Josh nodded, keeping his lips pursed and his eyes firmly on the screen. His suspended disbelief was dipping dangerously close to the ground; however small and rural this community was, the likelihood of their police force going off duty in its entirety to attend a party was slim. Still, he supposed, it wasn't an emergency, and they could be pursuing leads elsewhere. Could be. Probably weren't.

"I'll make sure we leave everything as we found it," Josh said, effectively dismissing Cosgrove from watching over him, but the man didn't take the hint. "Go and have a cup of tea, put your feet up."

Cosgrove smirked, bowed and retreated.

Josh turned back to the screen. "OK. Let's see what this button…no. I might delete it all by accident and be pseudo-arrested for destroying pseudo-evidence."

"Do you always talk to yourself?"

"Only when I'm craving stimulating, intellectual conversation," Josh replied, unfazed by Mark's stealthy arrival. To his credit, Mark chuckled agreeably.

"Josh, this is…"

"Trish," Mark's new associate provided.

"Hey, Trish."

"She designs security software," Mark said.

"Fancy that," Josh muttered, but neither Mark nor Trish picked up on his sarcasm. He couldn't understand why no-one else was suspicious, unless the joke was on him and they were all in on it. Whatever the reason, he wasn't about to spoil the illusion; he beckoned to the newcomer. "What do you make of this?"

She came over, eyes narrowed. "O…K. That's pretty old software, but the functions haven't changed much. May I?"

Josh got up from the stool and moved away. "Can I leave you to it?"

The answer was unequivocally yes—Trish already had black-and-white video feeds springing up all over the screen—but he waited for her to confirm it with a, "Yep, no worries," before he dodged past Mark and out of the grotty office, disheartened when he heard footsteps behind him.

"Hey," Mark said as he caught up. "How d'you feel about talking to the photographer?"

"I'd be happy to, but it won't help the investigation."

"Why—ah. Never mind. Privileged information, right?"

"Right." He'd have suggested Mark talk to him instead. However, assuming first of all that Clara really had been murdered—probability of 50%, give or take, depending on the moment—the last thing Matt needed was a tête-à-tête with a lawyer who had the finesse of a rampaging bull. On the other hand... "But he might appreciate the chance to talk to a therapist."

"I'd say so," Mark said. "It's very kind of you to offer and give up your free time." The man flung sincerity with expert precision, and it hit Josh right in the conscience.

"We should go back to the great hall, talk to a few of the others."

"No problem—I'll handle that. Why don't you go and ask your friend the butler if he'll take you to the photographer?"

Your friend the butler? What the hell is that about? Cosgrove was only doing his job. Nonetheless, they'd cover more ground if they split up and worked to their strengths. "In that case, let's reconvene in an hour."

"Great. See you then!"

***

Amber drew air through her teeth at the choice name a woman further down their table hurled at her partner. "I hope Mark and Josh get back here soon."

George nodded, thinking the same. The atmosphere in the great hall reminded him of the time in primary school when someone had let off a firework at morning playtime and the headteacher kept everyone in over lunch until the culprit came forward. A couple of fights had broken out, one after the other, like the start of a riot at a football match, before Andy Jeffries had owned up. Whether he'd done it of his own free will, they'd never know, but they were released for the last ten minutes of lunch break, riot averted.

It probably wouldn't go that far here, but the guests were restless, confined by boredom because, in this big house full of valuable junk, there was nothing to do, or nothing any of them wanted to do.

"You know what? They need a bar," George said.

"Yeah," Amber agreed. "And music."

George watched the serving staff, standing idle at the side of the hall, and then homed in on Gabby, sipping at her coffee and acting cool, calm and collected. She noticed him watching and smiled glibly. She was totally out of her depth.

"Be right back," George told Amber and set off around the tables to reach Gabby.

At some point, Andrew must have left; the chair next to hers was empty. George sat in it. "You OK?"

"I'm not sure how to keep them entertained. I thought they'd be fine just socialising."

"Well, yeah. That's what they'd be doing any other Saturday night." George gave it half a minute so it wasn't obvious he'd already sussed the problem and come over for that reason. "Can I make a suggestion?"

"Yes, please do."

"How much beer have you got?"

"We ordered two dozen crates when you asked for it earlier— you weren't the only one, incidentally. Why? What do you have in mind?"

"Can we move these tables?"

"Yes—oh! I see." She rubbed her forehead as if staving off a headache. "How stupid I am."

"No, Gab. You put together a great itinerary for this weekend."

"But they're not enjoying themselves."

"I disagree. Sleeping in a four-poster, being waited on hand and foot, getting two dozen crates of beer delivered at seven o'clock on a Saturday night—it's just so different to how most of us live, which is awesome, by the way. Don't change any of it. But maybe you could build in a bit of free time where people can let their hair down? It's kind of tiring keeping up appearances all day."

"Yes, I know that feeling all too well." Gabby sat back, humming thoughtfully as she surveyed the hall. "All right. I can fix this, I think." She looked over at the serving staff, who were immediately attentive; she mouthed 'one minute', then turned back to George. "Thank you for your honesty."

"I hope I didn't offend you."

"Not at all." She smiled mischievously. "Your husband already has that covered."

Chapter Seventeen

"I DO APOLOGISE, JOSH," Cosgrove said—again—as he accompanied him back to the great hall.

"Really, it's fine," Josh replied, no longer disguising his weariness. "It strikes me as strange that your staff didn't keep you apprised of the situation."

"Indeed, although I was rather busy assisting you and Mr. Cottrell, and the under-butler is more than capable of handling such matters."

True as that might have been, Cosgrove had taken Josh on what amounted to a wild goose chase, up to Clara and Matt's now-empty room. Apparently, Matt's girlfriend had come for him, which, whilst understandable—or at least plausible—in the circumstances, seemed an awfully convenient distraction. Josh was but one of fifty-nine...*fifty-eight* guests, and he didn't think he was particularly difficult to distract—just point him at a good book—whereas the rest...

"Well, would you look at that." Josh came to an astonished halt at the entrance to the great hall, as did Cosgrove. "Your staff didn't tell you about this either, did they?"

"No, they did not." Cosgrove spoke tightly, his lips thin and unmoving. "We appear only to be missing the boughs of holly."

Josh smirked, trying so very hard not to laugh. "Come on, I'll get you a drink."

" I don't think—"

"I insist."

Mumbling something about impropriety, Cosgrove followed Josh over to the makeshift bar—a table on the dais, behind which three of the serving staff smiled cheerfully as they popped the lids off beer bottles and handed them to guests as required. From somewhere, music played—a cathedral choir, by the sound of it, but it was Christmas music nevertheless.

"Josh!"

"Good grief." Three people had shouted him at once, and Mark reached him first, Techy Trish a step behind, looking both pleased with herself and frustrated. "Bad news?" Josh asked.

"Mixed. I've been through all the recordings, and it turns out there isn't a camera in the art studio."

Josh turned to Cosgrove and glowered rather than asking.

"That's correct," Cosgrove confirmed. "There are no cameras in either the east or the west wing."

"You could've told us earlier, before Trish wasted an hour trawling through video footage."

"Oh, it wasn't a waste," Trish said. "One of the external cameras picked up someone running towards the gardens just after six p.m."

"What time did Gab—sorry, Her Ladyship find Clara?"

"Six-fifteen," Cosgrove supplied.

"OK. So this man—"

Trish interjected. "It was dark, so you can't actually tell if it's a man."

"This *person*—did anyone see them?"

"Josh!" Gabby called again and beckoned him with unnecessary enthusiasm.

He sighed. "Excuse me one moment." Edging past Mark and Trish, he went over to where Gabby was standing. "Oh, hey, I didn't see you there."

George was crouched next to a sitting woman, his arm bent awkwardly to prop up a sketchpad whilst she sketched at speed, debating each stroke of the pencil with two other women looking over her shoulders.

"What's going on?" Josh asked.

"They saw this guy—" George nodded at the half-done drawing "—heading towards the village as they were on their way back."

"The security camera picked up someone too. Are you sure it was a man?"

Both women gave a hurried nod without pausing from their joint efforts. Josh moved around to the side of the chair so he could see the sketch the right way up. Then he dug his glasses out of his pocket and looked again. He met George's gaze. That wasn't just any man; it was Matt Shapiro.

***

"Jeez, this room's hot," George muttered and rested his arm on top of the filing cabinet he was pinned against. It didn't help that there were five other people in the tiny office. On the plus side, the filing cabinet, while dusty as a dirt track, was cool against his bare skin; he'd ditched his dress shirt some time ago and felt a bit more like himself. Better still, other guests had followed his lead and exchanged their formal dinner attire for more typical Saturday-night casuals and enough Christmas sweaters to render the decorations Cosgrove had bought redundant.

"It makes no sense," Amber said. They'd watched the same piece of CCTV footage—from the internal camera closest to the west wing—three times, keeping an eye out for any trace of movement, but there was nothing, not even a shadow.

"Would he definitely have to pass that camera to leave the building?" asked the new guy, who worked in security and either hadn't told them his name or George had missed it amid all the big-upping.

"Yes," Josh snapped, having answered the same question twice already. "I was standing right there!" He jabbed his finger near the screen to indicate the wall, which took up most of the camera's view, and then at the dark sliver of space on the right. "That's the only way out of the west wing."

"All right, just wanted to make sure—"

Josh shot him down with a death glare and turned his back on him.

To be fair to the guy, Josh and Mark were treating him like he was one of many candidates for a Very Important Mission when, actually, half the guests were happy drinking the night away. The other half were either conducting their own independent investigations or, if they'd been foolish enough to ask what they could do, were in one of several six-strong teams, each charged with searching a specific area of the house and required to reconvene in the great hall at 10:30 p.m. to report back.

It was all a bit mad. Still, everyone seemed to be enjoying the evening, or George hoped it was everyone; fake or real, the murder investigation had kind of hijacked their anniversary weekend, as he'd known it would. But at least, for once, they were in it together. That counted for something.

"This is pointless," Josh muttered and pushed his way between Mark and Amber, making a beeline for the door.

"Where are you going?" George called, but Josh was already out of sight. The others watched him leave and then all turned to look at George. He shrugged apologetically and went after Josh, who was striding away at such a speed George had to jog to catch up with him.

"I had a thought," Josh said as he marched on.

"OK?"

"What if Matt hasn't left?"

"Well, you're the one who said he had."

"The under-butler said he'd called Matt's girlfriend, and his belongings were gone from the room. But he could just have moved to a different room."

"Why don't you ask Cosgrove? He'll know."

"I wouldn't bank on it…" Josh stopped talking while they passed a group of guests clustered around a painting, one of whom was holding a pair of glasses up to it, using a lens as a magnifying glass. Josh shook his head and muttered, "Amateurs," which made George laugh. Josh turned and grinned.

"You were saying…" George prompted.

"Yes. I have a feeling the rest of the staff is under instruction to keep Cosgrove in the dark. To what end, I don't know."

They rounded the corner into the entrance hall and puttered to a standstill. "I do," George said.

Josh covered his mouth and gave a muffled squeak.

Holding a foot-wide gold star at arm's length and standing atop a stepladder next to a massive, mostly decorated Christmas tree, was Cosgrove.

Still with star in hand, he twisted to face them. The ladder wobbled. Josh gasped and pushed his face against George's shoulder, covering his eyes with George's T-shirt sleeve.

"He's scared of heights," George explained.

Cosgrove mouthed an 'ah'.

"Did you do all that by yourself?"

"Goodness, no!" a woman exclaimed, and then, chortling, Gabby's nanny stepped out from behind the tree. Josh chanced a peek, saw Cosgrove was still up the ladder, and hid his face again. George sighed—in sympathy. Phobias were debilitating, as he knew all too well.

Cosgrove hastily set the star in place and climbed down the ladder, which he folded and leaned against the wall, then took a step back and nodded at Martha, who momentarily disappeared behind the tree again. The tree lit up, and Martha reappeared, looking to Cosgrove in query.

"I do believe we're done, Mrs. Perkins."

"I do believe you're right, Cosgrove." Brushing her palms together, she went to stand with her former colleague and admire their handiwork.

George nudged Josh. "You can look now."

Cautiously, Josh straightened up and shook his hair back from his face. This time, it was a very different kind of gasp that escaped him. "Wow. It's beautiful."

"Yeah, it is," George said, already mesmerised by what had to be over a thousand twinkling gold lights reflecting off hundreds of tiny, pearlescent glass baubles. Josh's hand found his, and he heard him sniff. "Hey, what's wrong?"

"Nothing." Josh rested his head on George's shoulder, laughing and sobbing all in one. "Happy tears," he said.

"Happy tears," Martha repeated quietly, but as always, the sound bounced off the bare surfaces.

"I shall put the ladder away," Cosgrove said. "And return with sherry."

Martha patted his arm fondly. "For four," she advised.

He nodded and left with the ladder, while Martha approached George and Josh.

"I don't know how you did it." She addressed them both. "We've never had decorations in the hall before. And I don't mean just this hall—the entire house."

"Never?" Josh repeated.

"Never," Martha confirmed. "I tried to persuade Cosgrove when the children were young, for their sakes and ours. He wouldn't hear of going against Gabby's father. Yet here we are. You've breathed life into the old place." She gestured to the tree, although she was looking behind George and Josh. The group who'd been studying the painting came around the corner and almost walked into them.

"We've got another clue for you," one of the women said.

Josh peered down his nose at her. "From the painting?"

"Sorry? Oh! No, we were having an argument. Tom—" she thumbed at the guy standing next to her "—reckoned the bloke in the painting was dabbing."

"He was what?"

Three of the six demonstrated; Josh recoiled in horror. "And was he?"

"No. He was aiming a rifle at a deer."

George turned away and stared at the tree. The effort to contain his laughter was making his eyes water. Josh poked him in the side, but he was ticklish, so it didn't help at all.

"You said you have another clue, although…I should point out I'm not in charge here."

"I would disagree," Martha murmured close to George's ear. He nodded and mouthed *me too*. Josh poked him again.

"Yeah, so," the young woman said, "it can't be the photographer. We were having a look around after the workshop—"

"*When* after the workshop?"

"About six-ish? We saw him coming out of the east wing."

Cosgrove arrived with a tray carrying four full sherry schooners.

"Ooh, are those for us?" the woman asked, hand outstretched to take one.

"No," Cosgrove and Josh snapped in unison.

She pulled her hand back as if someone had slapped it and scowled. In retaliation, Josh picked up one of the glasses and raised it in a toast before sipping it with a bordering-on-sexual appreciative groan. He didn't even like sherry that much.

"Thanks for telling us," George said. "That's really helpful." He had no idea if it was or it wasn't, but he had to smooth things over somehow.

The woman beckoned her group with a jerk of the head and led them back the way they'd come, glancing over her shoulder several times to glare at Josh. He wasn't in the least bit bothered.

"Sherry, George?" Cosgrove held the tray closer.

He was in the process of pulling his phone from his pocket to check the time. "Thanks," he said, taking a glass and activating his phone screen. "Crap. It's almost half ten. We need to get back to the great hall." He put the glass back on the tray. "Maybe I can drink it with my cheese."

Cosgrove smiled in approval. "An excellent combination." He was gone before George could explain he'd been joking.

"Come on, Watson," Josh said. "Let's see if Inspector Gregson's made any progress. Mrs. Hudson, are you coming with us?"

Martha drank her sherry in one and put her glass down on the closest table. "Surely, Cosgrove is Mrs. Hudson. I'd much rather be…Moriarty."

"Holmes' nemesis," Josh mused as he walked and then stopped. "You're not the murderer, are you?"

Martha smiled mysteriously.

Chapter Eighteen

ALL RIGHT. WHAT else do we know about the victim?" Mark asked the assembled guests, who were a dozen times more attentive than Josh's best students, even those guests on the drunk side of tipsy. As detectives, though, they were next to useless. All they'd established was a time of death between quarter to and quarter past six and that a man, possibly Matt Shapiro—although he'd been seen exiting the east tower around the same time—was caught on CCTV, running across the gardens at 18:10, and was, potentially, the same man seen by two guests as he ran towards the local village.

In other words, they knew no more than they had before the 'briefing session', and all it had achieved was to convince Josh this was a hoax. Entertaining and elaborate, yes—he was particularly impressed by the planting of the news article—but still a hoax. No doubt Clara Coltrane was tucked up safe and warm in her own bed, deciding how to spend the handsome fee Gabby and Andrew had paid her.

But what did it matter? The guests were enjoying themselves—even Josh, if he was honest.

A timid-looking man near the back of the hall raised his hand, and Mark invited him to come forward. The man shook his head and stayed where he was.

"Go on," Josh encouraged. Mark was an excellent manager on the whole, if not a little inflexible in his approach, to the detriment of the less self-confident guests. There again, lawyers were assertive, if not downright aggressive, so dealing with introverts was probably all new ground for Mark.

"I've looked into Clara Coltrane's career," said the timid man. A few people muttered 'can't hear him'. He coughed and spoke a bit louder. "Before she took the job with *Country Life*, she had a column in the local paper here."

"Oh, did she?" Josh said. "That's…an intriguing lead."

The timid man became a little less so. "It was quite inflammatory too. She published an allegation that the parish priest was having an affair with the organist's wife. The paper later issued a public apology. On another occasion, she claimed the headteacher of one of the primary schools was dating a high school student. It cost him his career, and he sued the paper, and they fired Ms. Coltrane. That's when she started writing for *Country Life*. Her column is kind of a gossip column, and she's obsessed with infidelity."

"What a hypocrite," someone called out. Josh didn't see who.

"Why's that?" he asked.

"She and Shapiro are involved. They admitted it last year in one of the nationals."

Matt had to be at least twenty years younger than Clara, not that it mattered, but there had been mention of a girlfriend, and now Josh thought about it, the two of them sharing a room—albeit a twin—was a little odd. Merton Hall wasn't exactly short of space to accommodate them separately.

"So she's made a few enemies, including some of the locals. That's a lot of potential suspects with motive."

"It would help if we knew more about *how* she died," someone else said, prompting lots of noise in agreement from the others that stopped dead when someone spoke up from the back of the room.

"I can help with that."

As one, they turned and tracked Andrew's shuffled, rigid progress to the front of the hall. In his arms was an object in swaddling towel, which, judging by the way he held himself and tripped on the dais, was a bit more cumbersome than a newborn babe. He set the object on the table-cum-makeshift-bar and slowly rolled back the towel.

"At first, I thought I must have knocked it over. No-one else had been up there. But then I realised…it wasn't on its stand."

A communal gasp sounded as the towel tumbled over the edge of the table, hanging there like a sullied altar cloth upon which lay a telescope, its bloodied end glistening grimly under the decadent chandeliers.

"To confirm," Mark said, simultaneously addressing Andrew—witness for the prosecution—and enunciating to the room—the jury, "this is the telescope from the solarium in the east wing."

"Yes."

A murmur grew, expanded, rose to fever pitch, and Josh saw it: the moment the guests, en masse, connected the dots.

"We need to find that photographer," Mark said, then, "Hold on!" then, "Bollocks," because it was too late.

Josh pinched his nose and shut his eyes, and he stayed like that until the angry rabble had funnelled out of the hall. The din faded to near-silence, bar the distant echo of self-appointed leaders vying for supremacy. "Well done. You've just instigated a lynch mob."

"If he's guilty—"

"We need to call the police and hand over to them, but I shouldn't have to tell you that. You're a barrister, for God's sake." Beside them, Andrew was meticulously re-wrapping the telescope in the towel. "And *you* should have left that where you found it."

"I…panicked," Andrew stuttered. "I'll put it back. I remember exactly where it was."

"Great. Apart from the fibres in the blood, and blood on the towel…"

Andrew gathered the telescope in his arms, cradling it. "I don't know what to do."

"It's OK, Andrew," Mark comforted, apparently having remembered he wasn't here 'for the prosecution' and this wasn't the Crown Court. "We'll talk to the police together. The important thing is you didn't touch it with your bare hands…did you?"

"No."

"Then it'll all be fine." Mark put his arm around Andrew's shoulders and guided him down from the dais, continuing to offer quiet reassurance as they headed for the doors.

"Wait!" Josh called. They both stopped and looked back. "Andrew, were you in the east wing between five-thirty and six-thirty?"

"No," Mark answered for him. "He was at the pub with me."

"So the east wing was empty?"

Andrew shrugged, as much as he was able. "I don't know. Howie and the children might have been there. You should ask Gabby."

Except Gabby had been in the west wing, discovering the victim, therefore could not state for certain the whereabouts of her family. "OK. Thanks, Andrew."

Josh watched them leave and went over to join George and Amber—the only people left in the great hall. "Well, what do you make of all that?"

"Seems fairly cut and dry," George said. Amber nodded in agreement.

"Does it? What do you know about telescopes?"

"Um…aside from what they do?" George frowned. "I dunno. They're expensive?"

"Yes, and…?"

"They're heavy," Amber said.

"Bingo. Yet we're supposed to believe the murderer took the telescope from the top of the east tower, carried it all the way down the stairs, across the building, all the way up the stairs to the top of the west tower, bludgeoned Clara Coltrane, then carried it all the way back again without being caught on CCTV?"

"I see your point," George said.

"I don't," Amber admitted.

"It's a setup—the murder mystery we were promised."

"But…" Amber stared at the table on the dais, then at the doors, then at nothing in particular. "It was all over Twitter."

"That doesn't make it true. It would only take a couple of guests to tweet about it, and for those tweets to be retweeted." Josh twitched internally every time he said the word.

"OK, but you can't dismiss the BBC reporting it."

"British institution that they are, they're still fallible."

"The police were here."

"Actors from Andrew's university."

Amber shook her head. "Mark spoke to them. He'd have known."

"Like he knew you didn't want him to take promotion?"

She blushed and clasped her hands, covering her wedding band.

George shot Josh a severe warning glance, but it was unnecessary. He was already aware he'd gone too far.

"I'm sorry. I shouldn't have said it."

"It's OK," Amber said quietly. "I've been trying to find a way to broach the subject without him becoming defensive. Maybe it'll be easier now. He can be quite bullish, but he's a good man."

"Yes, and it's obvious he loves you very much."

"He does. He's just…impulsive, like before." She glanced to the doors again. "So you're sure Clara's not dead?"

"Almost certain," Josh said, "but if that mob finds Matt Shapiro, there *will* be murder in this house tonight."

***

They didn't find him. Whether he'd left earlier with his girlfriend or the staff had hatched an emergency escape plan, he was no longer in the building. Once they were over the thrill of the hunt and the disappointment of not finding their prey, the guests returned to the hall to finish their drinks and then retired to their rooms, satisfied they'd done all they could until morning. Or most were satisfied…

"D'you want the bathroom first?" George asked when they reached their room.

"Hmm?" Josh had on his deep-in-thought face.

"Bathroom?"

"Oh! No. You carry on."

George didn't need telling twice. He'd had a fair bit of beer, and while he didn't feel drunk, his bladder was ready to burst.

"Of course, if it is real," Josh said outside the door, "come morning, the police will take over anyway."

"I thought you said you were sure."

"Just keeping an open mind, George."

Open and busy, which didn't bode well for sleep, especially as Josh had only had a glass of sherry and was still sober enough to drive—not that they were going anywhere before tomorrow afternoon, and Josh's insomnia wouldn't stop George sleeping. After getting so little the previous night, and a six-mile hike on top, he was absolutely shattered. But he was also worried. They might have successfully solved the murder mystery, but Merton Hall held plenty more opportunities for nighttime mischief.

"Your cheese board's arrived," Josh said as they passed in the bathroom doorway.

"Ah. I'd forgotten about that." George spotted the tray on the dresser and went to investigate, smiling when he saw the schooner of sherry next to the plate of cheese. "Wanna share?" He peeled a corner off the hunk of crumbly Lancashire and put it on his tongue, letting it melt in his mouth. "Mmm, that's good." He broke off another piece, larger this time.

The toilet flushed, and Josh emerged, shirt half unbuttoned and belt buckle dangling. "Are you sure you want to?"

"Uh-huh. In bed, though."

"But the crumbs…" Josh protested. George muffled it with a kiss.

From there, they made short work of getting out of their clothes and under the duvet; it was too cold not to. George set the plate down between them and cut a piece of Brie, which, in the low temperature, held its integrity. He fed it to Josh straight from the knife. "I'm gonna have nightmares about cheese-eating gargoyles."

"Assuming cheese causes nightmares…"

"How do you know it doesn't? You never sleep."

"Not true. What's that blue cheese?"

"Stilton?" George cut a slice off the block and lifted it to smell it before he ate it, but Josh got there first and stole it from right under George's nose.

"Mmm. Yes. Stilton. More." The words vibrated against George's lips. He blindly chopped and held the resulting tiny pyramid of blue cheese between them, going for it at the same time Josh did so that each got a small morsel.

"More?" George murmured.

"Yes." Josh moved back to give him room to work. "You know in the DSM, one of the characteristics of autism spectrum disorder is difficulty engaging in imaginative play."

George groaned. "Do you ever take a day off?"

"I wouldn't be me if I did."

"Fair comment. What's your point?"

"It's not a valid indicator. Think about it. There are so many brilliant, successful autistic actors, and look at Andrew's performance tonight. It was absolutely stellar."

"Stellar, yep," George repeated with a grin. Josh frowned. "Telescope? Stars?"

"Oh! Ha-ha." He nodded at the cheese by way of requesting more. George obliged; it was the one food they both agreed was delicious.

"So, are we going with 'the photographer did it in the art studio…'"

"With a telescope," Josh finished. "Motive—"

"The girlfriend's a new development. Clara refused to end things, so Matt took the initiative."

Josh looked doubtful, and rightly so. George was making it up.

"You know the other thing I can't figure out? How he got the telescope back to the east wing."

"Why would he need to?" Josh asked.

George had to think about that one for a minute. "Oh, yeah. Well, I guess we'll find out in the morning whether we're right."

Chapter Nineteen

JOSH SOUGHT HIS phone out by touch and briefly activated the screen: 4:21. He deposited it back on the bedside cabinet and hastily tucked his arm under the duvet, trying to still his shivering in the absolute darkness. He couldn't fault the curtains on that score; now the wind had died down, their room was a study in sensory deprivation. Other than the cold.

It was bloody freezing, and he was wide awake. If he were at home, he'd get up and make a coffee, feeding himself the lie that he could always go back to bed later, until reasoning and problem-solving shoved aside the last remnants of dreams and he accepted he was up for the day. They were doing their damnedest to get him up and moving now, but what would be the point? The kitchen staff could already be hard at work, preparing breakfast, but they might not be, and he wasn't going to wake someone solely to cater to his insomnia.

So, no coffee, and he'd left his laptop at home—intentionally. He could read, he supposed, and risk frostbitten fingers…or he could try going back to sleep.

Well, that was doomed to failure before he even began, but begin he did, letting his mind fill with the events of the previous day. Frustratingly, he was still only ninety-nine percent sure Clara Coltrane was alive and well, and it came back to what Andrew had said about the murder mysteries being inspired by the real deaths in Merton Hall. The scenario they'd encountered was nothing like any of them; Josh knew, because he'd seen the records.

Had he missed something? Unlikely. There had to be some small detail he was overlooking. The last death was Gabby and Andrew's grandmother; cause: lung damage from inhaling white spirit, *not* a blunt-instrument head trauma. Or should they have asked Gabby for more details about what she'd seen? Was there a smell of white spirit in the studio? No. She'd delivered her clues and then stayed out of the way.

He rolled over and braved checking the time again: 4:38. So much for going back to sleep. His brain was firing on all cylinders now, and the more he thought about the murder mystery, the more sure he became that Gabby and Andrew had been priming him from the second he'd arrived, which meant his exclusive access to the library wasn't a thoughtful gift; it was part of their ploy. They'd wanted him to find something in there—something that would have convinced him the cursed art studio had struck again.

How naïve of them to think it would be that easy. How insulting! Well, I'm not playing their game anymore. I'm…

"Bugger." He sat up and rubbed his face. "Bugger and botheration." He switched on the bedside lamp. George stirred and reached behind him, patting Josh's leg. "What's he doing?" Josh muttered.

"Checking you're still in bed."

"Oh. OK." It was telling, if not a tad bizarre. "I won't be for much longer."

George rolled over and peered, one-eyed. "Time is it?"

"Almost five. I've had a thought."

"Hmph."

"Want to hear it?"

"Can it wait?"

"Of course it can." Josh pushed away the covers. "I'll tell you when I get back."

George sighed heavily. "Gimme a minute."

"You don't have to come with me."

"Yeah, I do." Still with eyes shut, George swung his legs off the side of the bed and sat up. "Where are we going?"

***

George glanced back at the blue and white 'POLICE DO NOT CROSS' tape. "If this *is* a real crime scene…"

"It's not," Josh said from somewhere far above.

"Why are we doing this again?" George muttered under his breath as he trudged up the stairs. If Josh was so sure the murder was staged, there was no reason to go sneaking around in the dead of night trying to figure out how the murderer escaped, which meant… "He's hunting another trail. Damn it." George quickened his pace, running the rest of the way to the top of the west tower, where Josh was waiting outside the art studio door. "Are you gonna explain at some point?"

Josh smirked and turned the doorknob. "Rapunzel, Rapunzel, let down your golden hair." He pushed the door open and activated the LED on his phone.

"There are lights, you know."

"I know, but this is more fun, don't you think?"

"Fun, yeah," George agreed drolly.

They both stood for a moment, surveying the room and the semicircle of easels, each bearing a painting. No signs of a struggle, no pool of blood; it looked exactly the same as when George had left the previous afternoon.

"Is that yours, on the end?" Josh shone the light on it and advanced, not quite on tiptoes.

"Yeah."

"Wow. Those shadows…so much depth…I could almost step into it. You're amazing!" Josh always gushed over George's paintings, but it still made him feel all warm and mushy. "How do you make the snow glisten like that?"

"Cad orange and white highlights." George went over and scrutinised his creation. He still had a couple of hours' work to do on it, minimum, but it was a lot better than he'd thought.

Josh had moved on and was standing in front of the cabinet, examining it closely and running his hands over the doors. He tried opening one, but it was locked. "What's in here? Do you know?"

"Art supplies," George answered cagily. He had a bad feeling about this—worse even than 'hey, let's just step right over this police tape and romp all over a potential crime scene'. "Why?"

Josh gestured at the lock. "Can you pick this?"

George reeled. "Are you serious?"

"Could you?"

"Um…if I had something to pick it with, probably. But—" Josh held out his hand, palm up. There was a paperclip on it.

George sighed. "And that just happened to be in your pocket, did it?"

"It did, honestly!"

"Yeah, right." He took the paperclip, straightening it as he turned to the cabinet and squinted at the lock. "I can't…never mind." He'd been about to say he couldn't see well enough, but with the help of the LED, he could see perfectly, more was the pity. "If I'd known what you were planning…" He reshaped the wire and poked it into the lock, twisting and easing it back and forth until he felt a springy resistance.

"I didn't plan, it's all improvised, but you'd have agreed just the same."

"Hmm." One turn and the lock clicked; George withdrew the paperclip and pulled the door open. "There. See? Just art supplies."

Josh flapped his hand to move him aside and opened both doors, then scooped everything off the top shelf and held it out to George. "Stick this lot somewhere."

"Joshua, what are you doing?"

"Emptying it. Look at the walls and tell me what you see."

"What do you want me to see?" George deposited the pile and returned for the next.

"How many doors?"

"One." And the next.

"Precisely."

"Huh?"

With the cupboard now empty, Josh bashed on the bottom of the top shelf and tugged it free. That, too, he handed to George. "Gabby said the battlements weren't accessible anymore."

"Right?" George propped the shelf against the wall.

"Well, they had to have been accessible at some point." Second shelf out; one more to go.

"Maybe they bricked up the doors?"

"Maybe," Josh said. He tugged the last shelf free. George stacked it with the others. "Or maybe they didn't and the doors are still here but concealed." He stepped into the cupboard, reached up, and then down.

"Are you m—" A blast of frigid air cut George's question dead. Astonished, he moved closer, looking past Josh's LED-illuminated silhouette to the snow-covered platform, no more than five feet wide but extending all the way to the east tower and framed by the gapped-teeth crenellations they'd only seen from below. "Whoa. What a view."

"Welcome to Narnia!" Josh glanced back, beaming with delight, and then stepped out of the cupboard. "Oh, shit!" With flailing arms, he fell forward.

George didn't think. He just made a grab for Josh, snatching handfuls of his sweater and hoisting him back into the room. "What happened? Did you slip?"

Josh was panting hard, maybe even hyperventilating. In the weird blue glow, he was almost as white as the snow on the battlements.

"Josh?"

He pointed the LED through the portal.

George didn't even move an inch before Josh grabbed his arm and yelled, "No!"

"I'm not going out there. I'm just gonna look."

"Be careful."

"OK…" Still with Josh clinging to him, George tentatively approached the doorway and looked down—

"Ah."

—into a black void.

***

"He could've jumped it," George reasoned. They were back in their room, having reconstructed the art studio cupboard and stopped by the kitchen for a medicinal brandy on the way. It was safe to say they wouldn't be going anywhere for at least another twelve hours.

"He couldn't," Josh said.

"It wasn't that wide a gap."

"No footprints. The snow was pristine."

"I'm happy to take your word for it." George hadn't noticed. His only concern had been to get that door safely shut, and no way was he going for a second look. "So if it wasn't about the murder, why did we just risk our lives? And what was that about Rapunzel?"

"Ah, yes. Gabby's great-grandmother. There's a portrait of her downstairs, possibly more than one, but in the one Gabby showed me, she had her hair in a long plait. She was blonde, nothing at all like Gabby and Andrew or their parents. She was also an artist and used to sneak her lover, Annabella, into the castle…house. God, those battlements." Josh downed his brandy and poured more into the glass. "Every time curiosity supersedes my fear, what happens? Never again. Never, ever again. Do you want to go back to bed?"

"I will, in a bit," George said. He couldn't stop yawning, but he wanted to be sure Josh wouldn't go off on another adventure if left unattended. "You think her lover got in through the battlements?"

"Well, I'm not suggesting she climbed Rapunzel's golden hair," Josh joked, although he was still too shaken for it to be funny or cutting, whichever of those he'd intended. "At some point, there must have been stairs either directly leading to the battlements or…ohhh! Inside the towers. That's it! There was a secret passage all along."

"Um…did I nod off there?"

Josh laughed. "No. I was thinking yesterday how much fun it would be to discover there was a secret passage into the library."

"That 'fun' word again…"

"Don't worry, George. I'm not going looking for it. If it's there, Andrew will know about it, which means he probably also knows his great-grandmother wasn't actually his great-grandmother."

"Let me guess this one," George said. "What was her name again? The lover?"

"Annabella." Josh narrowed his eyes. "She was a nurse."

"Figures," George said. "She'd have known a thing or two about pregnancy then, huh?"

"Yes, she would." Josh was fighting a grin. "Come on, George, stop being a smart alec and just say it."

"Annabella's their great-grandmother. Am I right?"

"You know damn well you are."

"Excellent!" George grinned.

"Elementary," Josh muttered dryly.

"Aw, don't be like that. You taught me everything I know."

"No, I was quoting Sherlock Holmes…well, Arthur Conan Doyle: 'It is one of those instances where the reasoner can produce an effect which seems remarkable to his neighbour, because the latter has missed the one little point which is the basis of the deduction. The same may be said, my dear fellow, for the effect of some of these little sketches of yours, which is entirely meretricious, depending as it does upon your retaining in your own hands some factors in the problem which are never imparted to the reader.'"

"Yeah," George nodded slowly, too tired to even *try* to understand any of what Josh had just said. "And on that note, I'm going back to bed." He shuffled out of his jeans and got straight under the duvet. "Don't do anything, OK?"

"Not even come back to bed with you?"

"You can do that." George shut his eyes, not thinking for a moment that Josh would do it.

A minute or so later, Josh curled up behind him. "Good night, ma moitié."

"Good night, Joshua. Again."

Chapter Twenty

"Good morning." Gabby appeared, perhaps a little the worse for wear but cheery, next to their breakfast table—not in the morning room today, but in the entrance hall. The formerly chilly and impersonal space was under the enchantment of the sight and scent of the tree, the snow-blanketed landscape beyond the picture window and piped orchestral Christmas music. "May I join you?"

"Please do," Josh invited.

She pulled out the chair next to George and diagonally opposite Josh, pausing for a member of staff to deliver a cup of black coffee. She smiled her thanks and sat, immediately picking up the cup and taking a sizable sip. "Triple espresso," she explained.

Josh raised an eyebrow. "Rough night?"

"I've had worse. How about you? Did you sleep well?"

"About the same as usual."

"I find it difficult myself, sleeping in a strange bed, no matter how comfortable."

Josh shifted his gaze to George, who frowned in query. There was something off about the conversation. "Gabby, did you still need my help?"

"No, but thank you. The detective inspector phoned at eight o'clock to say she'd be here within the hour. What are we?" She shook her sleeve back and looked at her watch. "Ten to nine, so any time now. All being well, they'll be done with the room before this morning's session is due to commence. She wants to check for signs of forced entry and dust for fingerprints. Apparently, something Matt Shapiro said suggested Clara interrupted a would-be burglar."

"A burglar?"

"Yes. Someone who was aware the west wing had minimal security. Of course, the only room with anything of value is the library, which has an excellent alarm system."

George picked up his fork and spun it back and forth across his empty breakfast plate. The worry lines extended to his scalp, and he was keeping his head down. Alas, Josh didn't have that luxury and had to meet Gabby's passive interrogation head on. She *knew* they'd been up to the art studio and was trying to coerce a confession out of them.

Guests began taking up their seats and giving their breakfast orders, the atmosphere on the whole jovial but pensive. Amber and Mark were among the last to arrive and waved to acknowledge Josh and George; they were coming over.

"Well, I must get on," Gabby said and rose from her chair.

"Are you going to debrief us?" Josh asked.

"As soon as I've spoken to the police." She turned, offered Amber and Mark a polite 'good morning' and continued swiftly on her way.

"Well, it wasn't anything we said," Amber remarked as she and Mark sat at the next table along.

"No," Josh said. "My fault again, I'm afraid."

"Oh?"

"You'll find out in due course, no doubt. Did you happen to notice any police officers on your way down?"

Amber and Mark looked at each other and shook their heads.

"I'm guessing our workshop won't go ahead," Amber said.

Josh smiled reassuringly. "Oh, everything will be done and dusted by then, I'm sure."

Mark scoffed. "Two hours to process a murder scene in a house this size?"

"If it *was* a murder," Amber said quietly.

"Of course it was! You saw the state Andrew was in." Mark wagged his finger at Josh. "This is down to you. You know that?"

"Excuse me!" Amber snapped. "I can make up my own mind, thank you!"

"Now look—" Mark began, trying to keep his voice down.

"Don't you talk to me like that." Her voice was equally low and twice as menacing.

Josh hid behind his hair, staying as still as could be, attempting invisibility—which George seemed to have already achieved—and almost wishing there had been a murder so he didn't feel responsible for the argument. But, as Amber said, she was capable of making up her own mind, and it wasn't as if Josh had lied to her nor even shared his opinion. He'd merely pointed out the evidence wasn't as conclusive as her husband seemed to think.

"Messrs. Sandison-Morley, your presence is required. Please, come with me."

"Your timing is impeccable," Josh murmured as he and George followed Cosgrove away from the entrance hall.

"As that may be, I'm simply following orders, sir."

Josh stayed quiet after that. He didn't like the return to the formal address, and by the time Cosgrove delivered them to their destination—the drawing room—he was beginning to think he was wrong; present were Gabby, Andrew and a tall, dark-suited woman, all three standing. Cosgrove bowed and retreated.

A silent minute dragged past, possibly longer; it was hard to tell.

"Why were we summoned?" Josh asked.

Still nobody spoke.

"OK. I admit it. I went up to the art studio in the early hours. Only me. George doesn't know anything."

"Liar," Gabby said—not an accusation. She looked over at the other woman. "Thank you, Stephanie. That will be all."

The woman nodded and marched, military-style, from the room.

Josh watched her leave. "Erm…" He stared at the door, then at Gabby, then at the door. Gabby snorted a laugh.

"My chauffeur."

"Your…" He trailed off, astounded.

"But thank you for owning up. Please, sit down. When Cosgrove returns, I'll get him to bring coffee. Is that all right, George? Or would you prefer herbal tea?"

"I'm f-fine…thanks." Those were the first words George had uttered since Gabby had left them at breakfast.

"I'm fine too," Josh confirmed. The sooner they got out of here, the better.

"As you wish," Gabby said. She and Andrew waited until Josh and George were seated, then sat, side by side, on a regency-striped, swirly-legged chaise longue—the sort upon which Oscar Wilde would have delighted in flinging himself.

"First things first," Gabby began. "Did we at any point convince you Clara Coltrane had been murdered?"

"No," Josh answered honestly, "but you made me question it many times."

"Oh, jolly good." That seemed to delight her.

"What about Mark?" Andrew asked. "Did he believe it?"

"He still does. He and Amber are presently arguing it out."

"Fantastic!"

"He doesn't mean their argument," Gabby qualified. "Do you?"

"Goodness, no."

"And the art studio?" Josh asked. "Do you really believe it's cursed?"

Gabby folded her arms, rested her index finger on her lips, and stared into space, hamming up the performance of deep pondering. No, she didn't believe it was cursed, as well he'd known, but she was considering how to answer. Josh decided to help her along.

"Let's skip past the bit where you tell me what Xander thinks."

She laughed. "Of course I don't, but what I do *know* is artists are sensitive, expressive beings, whose experience of pain and anguish is more intense than *most* non-artists could ever imagine."

"Then we are in accord." Josh sought out George's hand, cherishing the security and familiarity as their palms slid into position and their fingers interlocked. "So everything else was misdirection," he concluded, but both siblings shook their heads, all smiles. "It wasn't? Well…" Josh did a quick rerun in light of Gabby's confirmation that it was the promised murder mystery, but he couldn't quite get there. "Can someone help me out here?"

"They wanted to keep you guessing," George said.

"Yes," Gabby confirmed.

"Doesn't that defeat the purpose? Surely, you must know I'd have gone along with it, regardless of whether I sussed within the first thirty seconds that it wasn't real, for the sake of the rest of the guests?"

"Oh, absolutely, and I'm tremendously grateful to you for not spoiling it for everyone else. I knew a fictitious murder mystery wouldn't hold your interest, and we didn't think we'd pull off fooling you that an actual murder had taken place. So we aimed for plausibility."

"You wanted us to try to establish if it was real," Josh realised.

"I wanted you to enjoy yourselves," Gabby said. "Have you?"

"Yes, very much."

"George?"

"A weekend of chasing wayward dogs and husbands? Yeah, it's been *fun*." He gave Josh a sideways grin.

"And painting," Josh added. "Don't forget the painting."

"Yes, indeed," Gabby said.

"I *loved* painting," George assured her. "Can't wait to crack on with it this morning." Gabby smiled her gratitude.

"What about Clara and Matt?" Josh asked.

"Alive and well and waiting in the wing…" She raised an eyebrow; Josh groaned at the pun. She laughed and finished, "For the big reveal."

"And are they still going to run their piece on your *Art of Murder* weekend? Or was that part of the act?"

"Art of Murder…" Gabby mused. "I really like that. May we steal it?"

Josh shrugged. "By all means."

"Thank you. And in answer to your question, yes, the piece will go ahead. For all that Clara is an insufferable hack, she's very fond of my parents and they of her."

"Figures," Josh muttered.

"I'll be sure to send you a copy," Gabby said with a smirk. "Anyway, I've kept you long enough, and Andrew needs to have the same conversation with Mark and Amber. I hope you're not awfully cross with me."

"Cross? Why would we be?"

"The deception."

"I see. Yes." It hadn't been the romantic weekend away Josh had planned, but that was down to George's love of lesser beasts and his own penchant for getting caught up in life-threatening drama in the pursuit of answers. Neither of those were Gabby's fault, but he understood why she'd thought they—or rather, he—might be cross.

He shrugged. "It wouldn't have worked without the deception, and it's not as if you made us do anything we wouldn't have done anyway. As far as I'm concerned, it's all present and ethically correct."

"So we're OK?"

Josh smiled. "We're OK."

Gabby sighed in relief.

"I do need to talk to the two of you, though, about your g—" Josh drew breath sharply at the sudden pain in his ankle.

"About?" Gabby prompted.

"Erm…guest rooms. You should provide coffee in the rooms."

"Oh. Well…look, would you like to stay for dinner? I know it's your anniversary…"

Josh and George both nodded, no need for private discussion. "We'd love to," Josh confirmed.

"Wonderful. I'll let your butler know."

"*Our* butler?"

Gabby smiled impishly. "That Christmas tree made a world of difference—to everyone. Dinner is the least we can do."

The drawing room door opened, and Amber and Mark stepped in; Josh imagined he and George had looked equally bamboozled when they'd been brought here.

"We'll leave you to it." Josh released George's hand, and they both rose from the sofa.

"All right. We'll be out to debrief all of our guests shortly, but we wanted to talk to the four of you first, primarily because you're our friends, but also because if we can keep the two of you entertained—" she peered over her glasses at Josh and then Mark "—anyone else is a breeze."

Epilogue

A TOAST." GABBY RAISED her glass. "To our inaugural—"

"Highly successful," Josh amended.

"Inaugural *and* highly successful Art of Murder weekend."

The multiple *tings* of lead crystal goblets rang through the air.

Josh raised his glass to Martha, sitting directly opposite and too far away to reach. To her left, slightly out of sorts and garbed in forest-green, chunky—what probably, for him, passed as a Christmas—sweater was Cosgrove. Josh would have used every mind-hack in his arsenal to persuade the man to accept his dinner invitation, but ultimately Gabby had intervened with a well-aimed 'oh, but I insist', to which Cosgrove had mumbled, 'As you wish, Your Ladyship.'

"Also, Happy Anniversary to Josh and George."

Another clang of glasses was accompanied by repeated utterances of 'Happy Anniversary'. Josh and George said thank you—a lot—and then looked at each other and started to laugh.

"You're blushing," George said, pressing the back of his hand to Josh's very warm cheek.

"So are you," Josh pointed out, and they shared a quick, bashful kiss.

"You'll have to up your Christmas game next year," Howie said to Gabby and Andrew. "Get some mistletoe around the place."

Gabby dismissed the idea with light laughter but glanced upward nonetheless.

"How long have you been married?" Andrew asked.

"Two and a half years," Josh said, then, before Andrew's brain got caught in a loop of *does not compute*, explained, "We had to bring our wedding forward for not very happy reasons, so we prefer instead to celebrate the anniversary of the day we proposed to each other."

"Oh, how lovely!" Martha gushed.

"And ever so romantic," Gabby added.

"See, Joshua?" George said with a grin. "Told you it was."

"Erm…no, actually, I told you."

"When?"

"On the way here."

"I don't remember that."

"Well, I did."

"You're making it up," George accused in jest, but Gabby's expression was one of mild alarm, so Josh let their audience in on the joke.

"We were discussing on the way here how romantic it would be to spend our anniversary in a rustic manor house, which turned out to be a castle with no heating in a snowstorm, but still… We've had a wonderful time. Thank you, Gabby and Andrew." Josh raised his glass to them, and everyone else followed his lead.

Gabby nodded modestly in thanks. "Well, I suppose the real test is…would you come again?"

"Try and stop us!" George said.

Gabby reached for his hand but couldn't quite stretch far enough without dipping her sleeve into Josh's dinner. "What about you?" she asked him.

"Depends," he said, attempting nonchalance. "Could I spend the entire weekend in the library?"

She peered at him over her glasses. "If you so desire."

Josh held her gaze for several moments, until he was sure that both of them were *not* saying the same thing: they'd enjoyed each other's company and would make a concerted effort to share it more often.

"We should eat," Gabby said, easing out of the moment to gesture at the spread before them. She'd lost the coin toss this time, thus was at the head of the table, but she filled the position well, and not because she'd been born to it. For the first time since they'd arrived at Merton Hall—indeed, for the first time in all the years he and Gabby had known each other—Josh sensed in her a calm acceptance of who she was and the responsibilities her role bestowed upon her.

"You too," she said, directing his attention to the plate in front of him. Josh obediently picked up his cutlery.

The meal was by far the best they'd had all weekend—in both Josh's *and* George's opinion: good old straightforward roast beef and Yorkshire pudding with roast potatoes, a colourful array of seasonal veg—Josh stuck to carrots and left the kale and red cabbage to the more adventurous diners, hence everyone else—served with rich, dark gravy. Dessert was a sweet, Armagnac-laced apple pie topped with frangipane and a drizzle of vanilla cream. It was all too delicious, and Josh ate until he literally couldn't swallow another mouthful. Meanwhile, George had seconds.

They took their after-dinner coffee in the drawing room, or all except Andrew and young Xander, who went off to stargaze, and Amber and Mark, who'd left before dinner to get back to their children. The curtains were closed, and a log fire flickered, lending some very welcome warmth and plenty of ambience. Cosgrove lingered near the hearth, surreptitiously adding a log as required—noticed by everyone, but he was happy, so they let him be—while Gabby and Martha gossiped outrageously about people Josh had never heard of, and Harriet interrogated George about his time on the ranch—specifically with the horses, as she competed in dressage—ignoring Howie's occasional pleas for her to stop pestering.

Tucked in the corner of the terribly upright sofa, Josh was content to just watch and listen, aware that across the room, Cosgrove was doing the same. He caught the other man's eye and went over to join him.

"I must thank you again for your assistance this weekend."

"It's been a pleasure," Cosgrove said, rocking on his heels. Not quite the truth, not quite a lie.

"Did I get you in trouble?"

"A little, but it was a worthwhile cause." He inclined his head toward Gabby, who'd taken off her glasses to dry her eyes from laughing. "Now, that is a rare sight."

Josh continued watching her while she was too engrossed to notice, and the longer he watched, the more certain he became that his theory about Annabella was correct. But George had been right to kick him, even if it had left a bruise. There was nothing useful to be gained from telling Gabby and Andrew they descended from a surrogate—and a commoner, at that—although Josh intended to fully utilise his open invitation to the library to find out more about Annabella and Gabby's great-grandmother. Had her great-grandfather known? Had he killed his wife for her infidelity? Or had he condoned it? Had the three shared a life of intimacy? Of course, none of that information would have been recorded, but the devil was always in the details.

"Penny for them," Gabby murmured, drawing up on his other side.

"Planning my next visit to your library."

"Your Ladyship, Josh…" With a bow, Cosgrove excused himself and went to gather the empty cups.

"The man is incorrigible," Josh remarked.

"And encourageable…" Gabby nudged him playfully. "It's lucky my father isn't here. He has no tolerance for insubordination, but you know that."

Josh nodded. "Yes, I do."

"Any regrets?"

"None."

"Glad to hear it. Ah, your husband has escaped," Gabby observed as George came over. "Has she talked your ear off?"

"No, it's cool. She's a great kid."

"She has her moments," Gabby said. "But don't they all?"

George chuckled. "Yep. Speaking of which…" He looked at Josh. "We should get going soon."

"Good idea." Josh checked what Cosgrove was up to—talking to Martha to disguise that he was loading the tray. "We need to get our case."

"I believe it has already been brought down," Gabby said. "Before you go, however, I do need a quick word with George."

George frowned. "OK?"

"It's nothing bad, I promise. The painting is just beautiful, thank you so much—again. Now I understand why you were so fired up after you'd been to the forest. You really are an incredibly talented artist."

George smiled coyly. "I'm glad you like it."

"I adore it, which is why I wanted to ask how you'd feel about licensing it for reprinting."

"It's yours, Gab. You can do what you like with it."

"I'd never presume, George. Of course, I'd ensure we have the necessary legal documentation—to cover your rights as much as ours."

"You don't need to do all that."

"But I do. You're right about the forest. It needs protecting, so tomorrow, I'll contact the Forestry Commission and find out what we need to do. Then, in the New Year, Andrew and I are going to meet with our parents, formally, to discuss taking over the management of the estate.

"That's what they've been waiting for—marking time until we came of age, and what did we do? We ran away as fast as we could. But this weekend has been…well, life-changing, quite frankly. We finally feel ready to make a go of this, and we have so many ideas—leasing the great hall for weddings and balls, renting out the art studio, a restaurant in the morning room, maybe even open the house as a hotel, which will mean employing a new hospitality staff…"

"What will happen to Cosgrove?" Josh asked, horrified that his interfering for Gabby's benefit might have cost his 'accomplice' his job.

"I've already spoken to him. He's five years away from retirement age, so he'll stay on here until our parents permanently move out, and they will, then he'll come to Porter Lodge to work for us until he decides he's had enough. Of course, nothing's set in stone until we have our parents' agreement, but I'll look after him, you have my word, even though you did lead him astray."

"We were merely adding a few finishing touches," Josh said, expecting another kick at any second. "Seriously, though, we've had a fabulous time this weekend, haven't we, George?"

"Yep. It's been awesome."

"And that's all yours and Andrew's doing," Josh added.

Gabby nodded meekly in acceptance of his praise. "True as that may be, we owe you both a debt of gratitude for showing us there's life in the old place…" There was nothing meek about that smirk, though. "And for breaking the curse."

***

"Nope, that's worse." George opened his eyes again, blinking away the blurriness, God only knew why, because now he was staring into the tunnel of white ahead of them. Much as Josh was a very able and experienced motorist and George trusted his driving more than anyone's, passenging along unlit roads covered in snow compacted by wind and frozen rain was the most terrifying experience of George's life.

"Put the radio on," Josh suggested.

"Can't." No way was he letting go of that grab handle. He'd rather— "Josh!"

"George, for goodness' sake. It's really not that bad."

"Just…keep hold of the steering wheel."

"I did."

"With both hands."

"And if I need to change gear?"

George clenched his teeth. His jaw ached already, and they'd only been in the car ten minutes.

"Are you warm enough?"

"Hmm-hmm."

"Not too warm?"

"Mmm-mmm." He was. The blowers had been on full blast since they left Merton Hall, but Josh wouldn't have even thawed out yet.

"We'll be on the motorway before you know it," Josh said. "And it'll be clear and well gritted."

"Yeah. The snow's probably only on the hills anyway."

"Exactly. You watch, when we get to sea level, there'll be none at all."

George sighed. "Back to normality."

"You sound sad."

"I guess I am a bit." George spotted approaching headlights and shut his eyes again. He really didn't need to see how the two vehicles were going to get past each other. He listened to the engine shifting down through the gears and then back up before he chanced opening his eyes again.

"OK," Josh said. "Truth time."

"Go on," George invited.

"Did you really enjoy yourself or were you just saying it for Gabby's and my benefit?"

"I really enjoyed myself."

"Even the bit where we nearly fell to our deaths from the battlements?"

George shrugged—such as he could when his shoulders were so tense he no longer knew where they ended and the car seat began. "I expected it, or not exactly that. I'm not psychic, and before you say it, I know. I was joking. But you were bound to get yourself in some kind of bother. You wouldn't be you if you didn't."

"You say the sweetest things."

George glanced over at Josh, just making out his smile in the glow from the dashboard. "Thank you for remembering to take me along for the ride—even if we did nearly fall to our deaths from the battlements."

"At least we'd have died together."

"Gee, that's cheery."

"See, now, if they'd had some of those gold ropes…"

"In an art cupboard?"

"I didn't see a single one in the entire building."

"No, but I bet they have them next time."

Josh slowed the car to take a hairpin bend, and they passed through the hamlet with the church and all the lights. It felt more Christmassy this time around, George wasn't sure why—perhaps because they were on their way home. Theirs might only be a tiny terraced house, but it was filled to the well-insulated rafters with love.

"So did you like the taste of the high life?" They were back to driving through the pitch-dark again, and Josh had only asked to distract him.

"Hmm…I dunno. I mean, I didn't miss washing up, and it was an eye-opener seeing how the other half live, but I couldn't stand it all the time. Butlers and servants and chauffeurs—"

"You have a chauffeur," Josh pointed out.

"Ha-ha. Then you've got a cook."

"I have," Josh agreed. "And I can categorically state that I like his cooking the best."

"You do, huh?"

"I do."

The road wound on, still icy, treacherous, low visibility. Still with George clinging onto the grab handle for dear life.

"So, haggis for Hogmanay, then?" he joked.

"On one condition."

George waited, and waited. They came up on the sign for the motorway. Josh indicated.

"You sing Robert Burns' version of 'Auld Lang Syne'."

"Damn it." He'd walked straight into that one.

No, George, it's really nice…interesting texture, isn't it?

On the other hand, haggis.

"Aye, but I'll have none of your haiverin'."

"George Sandison-Morley, I didn't think it was possible to love you more." Josh reached across the centre console. George batted his arm away.

"How about with both hands *on the wheel*."

The End

Acknowledgements

Amy, Andrea, David, Kaje, Jor (because you'll have proofread it anyway) and Nige – thank you! I threw this one at you at the last minute. I'll try to not do it again. ;)

Quotations used are from the following works, all in the public domain:

Robert Burns (1786), 'To a Mouse, on Turning Her Up in Her Nest With the Plough, November, 1785'. Scottish Poetry Library. Available at https://www.scottishpoetrylibrary.org.uk/poem/mouse/

Robert Burns (1787), 'Address to a Haggis'. Scottish Poetry Library. Available at https://www.scottishpoetrylibrary.org.uk/poem/address-haggis/

Charles Dickens (1840, 2014), *The Posthumous Papers of the Pickwick Club*. Available at https://www.gutenberg.org/ebooks/47534

Arthur Conan Doyle (1893, 1997), 'Adventure VII. The Crooked Man' in *The Memoirs of Sherlock Holmes*. Available at https://www.gutenberg.org/ebooks/834

About the Author

Debbie McGowan is an author and publisher based in a semi-rural corner of Lancashire, England. She writes character-driven, realist fiction, celebrating life, love and relationships. A working-class girl, she 'ran away' to London at seventeen, was homeless, unemployed and then homeless again, interspersed with animal rights activism (all legal, honest ;)) and volunteer work as a mental health advocate. At twenty-five, she went back to college to study social science—tough with two toddlers, but they had a 'stay at home' dad, so it worked itself out. These days, the toddlers are young women (much to their chagrin) and Debbie teaches undergraduate students, writes novels and runs an independent publishing company, occasionally grabbing an hour's sleep where she can.

Social Media Links

Website: debbiemcgowan.co.uk and hidingbehindthecouch.com
Newsletter Signup: eepurl.com/b8emHL
Blog: deb248211.blogspot.com
Facebook: facebook.com/DebbieMcGowanAuthor and facebook.com/beatentrackpublishing
Twitter: @writerdebmcg
YouTube: youtube.com/deb248211
Instagram: instagram/writerdebmcg
Tumblr: writerdebmcg.tumblr.com
LinkedIn: uk.linkedin.com/in/writerdebmcg
Goodreads: goodreads.com/DebbieMcGowan
Books2Read: books2read.com/DebbieMcGowan

By the Author

I'm not a single-genre author, for which I make no apology. Nor do I write stories of a specific length; I believe a story should be as long as it needs to be.

Thus, to assist you in navigating my catalogue, I've also included the closest-fitting genres and types of publication.

Hiding Behind The Couch Series
(Contemporary/Literary Fiction)

The ongoing story of 'The Circle'...
Nine friends from high school;
Nine friends for life.

The Story So Far...
(in chronological order)

- *Beginnings* (Novella)
- *Ruminations* (Novel)
- *Class-A* (Short Story – also in *Take a Chance* anthology)
- *Hiding Behind The Couch* (Season One)
- *No Time Like The Present* (Season Two)
- *The Harder They Fall* (Season Three)
- *Crying in the Rain* (Novel)
- *First Christmas* (Novella)
- *In The Stars Part I: Capricorn–Gemini* (Season Four)
- *Breaking Waves* (Novella)
- *Chain of Secrets* (Novella – also in Love Unlocked anthology)
- *In The Stars Part II: Cancer–Sagittarius* (Season Five)
- *A Midnight Clear* (Novella – also in *Boughs of Evergreen* anthology)
- *Red Hot Christmas* (Novella)

- *Two By Two* (Season Six)
- *Hiding Out* (Novella – CHO Crossover)
- *Those Jeffries Boys* (Novel)
- *The WAG and The Scoundrel* (Gray Fisher #1)
- *Perfect Tenor* (Novella)
- *The Lost Mitten* (see 'Children's Stories')
- *Reunions* (Season Seven)
- *Tabula Rasa* (Gray Fisher #2)
- *Breakfast at Cordelia's Aquarium* (Short Story)
- *Reverberations* (Novel)
- *To Be Sure* (Novella – also in *Never Too Late* anthology)
- *What A Scorcher!* (Flash Fiction)
- *Goth of Christmas Past* (Front of House #1)
- ***The Advent of Reason* (Novella)**
- *Not My Christmas* (Novella)
- *Highlights* ~ co-written with A.M. Leibowitz (Short Story – Notes from Boston meets Hiding Behind The Couch)
- *Distractions* (Gray Fisher #3)

Checking Him Out Series
(M/M and LGBTQ Romance)

- *Checking Him Out* (Book One)
- *Checking Him Out For the Holidays* (Novella)
- *Hiding Out* (Novella – Noah and Matty – HBTC Crossover)
- *Taking Him On* (Book Two – Noah and Matty)
- *Checking In* (Book Three)
- *The Making of Us* (Book Four – Jesse and Leigh)

Seeds of Tyrone Series
(M/M Romance)

~ co-written with Raine O'Tierney

- *Leaving Flowers* (Book One)
- *Where the Grass is Greener* (Book Two)
- *Christmas Craic and Mistletoe* (Book Three)

Stand-Alone Stories

- *Champagne* (LGBTQ Historical Novel)
- 'Time to Go' (Contemporary Short in *Story Salon Big Book of Stories*)
- *And The Walls Came Tumbling Down* (Sci-fi Novel)
- *No Dice* (Sci-fi Novel)
- *Double Six* (Sci-fi Novel)
- *Sugar and Sawdust* (M/M Romance Short Story)
- *Cherry Pop Valentine* (M/M Romance Short Story)
- *Coming Up* ~ co-written with Al Stewart (LGBTQ Short Story)
- *Of the Bauble* (LGBTQ Fantasy Romance Novella)
- *So Long, Little Black Diamonds* (True Short Story)
- *The Pastor's Last Drop* (Ongoing Historical Novel – Wattpad)
- *When Skies Have Fallen* (LGBTQ Historical Romance Novel)
- *A Snowy Ball* (When Skies Have Fallen Novelette)
- *The Great Village Bun Fight* (LGBTQ Comedy Novella – also in *Seasons of Love* anthology)
- 'Oh No She Didn't!' (LGBTQ Short Story in *Upstaged!: an anthology of women who love women in the performing arts*)
- *The Great Pretendo* (Flash Fiction)
- 'Nina, Pretty Ballerina' (Short Story in *Play On…: a collection of short stories, poetry and prose, inspired by the songs of ABBA*)
- *Meredith's Dagger* (Contemporary/Historical Feminist/LGBTQ Novel)

Audiobooks

- *And The Walls Came Tumbling Down* – Narrated by Hannibal Mills
- *Checking Him Out* – Narrated by Tim Larkfield
- *Of The Bauble* – Narrated by Jack Hardman
- *The Great Village Bun Fight* – Narrated by Jack Hardman
- *When Skies Have Fallen* – Narrated by Tim Holbourne

Children's Stories (written as J.S. Morley)

- *The Lost Mitten* ~ illustrated by Sofia Oxelstrand
- *Chompy the Velociraptor* ~ illustrated by Kate Andrew
- *Zoom the Pterodactyl*

www.debbiemcgowan.co.uk

Beaten Track Publishing

For more titles from Beaten Track Publishing,
please visit our website:

https://www.beatentrackpublishing.com

Thanks for reading!